When a horseman rides into camp, with a bullet hole in his gut and not long for this world, Will Jones finds not only that the dying man has a gang of New South Wales mounted police on his tail, but a canvas-wrapped parcel in his saddle bags. A scrawled address includes the promise of a reward to deliver the package to a station-owner in Western Queensland.

With two mates, and an unexpected hanger-on, Will sets out on an adventure across two lawless states in 1880s Australia. Yet, he soon learns that there is a price on his head, and that he is an unwitting tool in a game with mysteriously high stakes.

Also by Greg Barron

HarperCollins Publishers Australia
Rotten Gods
Savage Tide
Lethal Sky
Voodoo Dawn (short fiction)

Stories of Oz Publishing
The Hammer of Ramenskoye (short fiction)
Camp Leichhardt
Galloping Jones and Other True Stories from
Australia's History
Whistler's Bones
Red Jack and the Ragged Thirteen
Outlaw: The Story of Joe Flick
The Time of Thunder
The Last Days of Dom Sebastian

Will Jones

and the
Dead Man's Letter

a novella by

Greg Barron

First edition published 2021
by **Stories of Oz** Publishing
PO Box K57
Haymarket NSW 1240

ABN: 0920230558
facebook.com/storiesofoz
ozbookstore.com

The right of Greg Barron to be identified as the author of this work has been asserted by him in accordance with the Copyright Amendment (Moral Rights) Act 2000

ISBN: 978-0-6453511-0-1

Cover Art and Design: Angus Crowley
Proof Reading: Brad Connors
Typeset in 11-point Book Antiqua
Printed and bound in Australia by IngramSpark

To Australian author Don Douglas,
who inspired me to write this story.

1

JOHN CLARKE rode into the river clearing with his spurs bloodied and his horse near lame, its ribs so bony you could hold a straw between them. The rider's eyes had sunk like sandstone caves into his skull. It seemed to Will Jones, who was watching him come, that Clarkie had come off second-best in a fight – most likely with the New South Wales Mounted Police.

Across the smoking fire Fat Sam laid aside the Cantonese-language book he had been reading, snatched his Snider carbine from the blanket beside him, and drew it up onto his lap, thumb on the hammer. Gamilaroi Jim, who was washing saddle cloths in the waterhole, took a few steps towards the crook of a paperbark tree where his weapon was leaning.

Clarkie rode on up to the fireside, swaying a little in the saddle, then pushed his hat back on his head. He opened his mouth to speak, then slowly fell sideways off the saddle to the ground, his right foot tangled in the stirrup until the horse tiredly kicked it away and headed for the water.

'What in blazes?' exclaimed Will Jones as he came to his feet. He stood at above-average height, with a clean jawline, shaved often enough to show a dimple in his chin. His eyes were warm blue, and he carried himself with easy grace. The cuffs of his moleskins were tucked into leggings, and his dark serge jacket was distinctive – won in a game of cards from a Royal Navy officer on shore leave from a ship-of-the-line anchored off Garden Island, Sydney, two years earlier.

Wearing that garment, now frayed at the sleeves and hems, Will went hustling across the dust. He kneeled at Clarkie's side, seeing the vacant eyes and slack lips, feeling for a pulse in his carotid before looking across at Fat Sam, whose dark eyes showed no sign of emotion, scarcely even interest.

'He's dead, I think,' said Will.

Sam, who was not really fat, just of that round-headed, short-limbed kind of build that can make a man seem that way, came to his feet and, still carrying the carbine, shuffled to the other side of the corpse. Sam laid aside his weapon and leaned down so his ear hovered close to the man-in-question's mouth. He listened intently then pressed his lips together and inclined his head gravely, 'Clarkie all-up finish.'

Continuing his investigations Sam pointed to a circle

of blood lower down on the man's shirt. With two dexterous hands he unfastened the lower part of the garment. A small entry wound was located below Clarkie's ribcage — a puckered little hole with bloody lips.

Together they turned him over and found no exit wound on the other side. The slug had expended all its energy inside, breaking up on bone. It seemed to Will that it was a miracle he had managed to ride at all.

'What a cow of a thing to happen,' he said.

He turned to where Gamilaroi Jim, wearing his usual garb of a pair of dungarees and no shirt, but carrying his rifle, was walking towards them.

'Hey Jim,' said Will. 'Clarkie's been shot. Can you run up that knoll yonder and check no traps are after him? The last thing we need is company.'

Jim came close enough to talk but kept his distance from the body. 'Sure thing, bloke. But he always were a risky barsted.'

Will looked down at the body and sighed. John Clarke was not really a mate, but he had ridden with them now and then. He and Will had panned a claim on the Turon for a few months back in the seventies and done a season of sheep mustering on Kinchega Station. They shared a love of good horses, whoever the owner happened to be, an aptitude for hard work when the need arose, and an aversion to authority. Yet Will had never quite trusted him.

Now, while Jim tackled the lower slopes of the trachyte peak nearby, Will began to go through Clarkie's pockets. There was nothing much of note, just a few cartridge caps, some coins and a small folding knife. These items quickly transferred ownership, and when this was done Will's eyes turned to the horse that was now drinking from the billabong, fetlock deep in water. She was a bay mare, that must scarcely weigh more than the man she had borne.

The mare tried to shy away when she heard Will coming, but he made soothing noises in his throat and managed to grasp the reins and lead her back out of the shallows.

'We'll just get this saddle off you, girl, and then you can go find some grass.'

Will unbuckled the girth, lifted the saddle down to the ground, then removed her bridle. With a hand resting lightly on her neck he said, 'You're free, off you go.'

The creek was an unnamed tributary of the Castlereagh, with some good waterholes and nourishing feed in the right season. The mare would either make her way back to wherever she had been stolen from or join a brumby herd. Either way Will wished her the best of luck.

The horse having wandered off, Will kneeled beside

the saddle while Sam, who was back on his blanket at the fireside, watched with interest.

First, Will unpacked the saddlebags. No food. No money. But some other items of interest. A .36 calibre squirt. Will sniffed the barrel, and the gunpowder smell was stale, not fresh. The final item was a canvas package, stitched closed, and sealed with wax on the seams. It was the size of a quarter-loaf of bread, and in neat letters the following words had been painted on its face.

WHOMSOEVER WILL DELIVER THIS PACKAGE UNOPENED TO JOE MCCARTNEY AT KYUNGRA STATION WILL BE GIVEN A REWARD OF ONE HUNDRED POUNDS. IT IS FULL RESTITUTION OF ALL DEBTS OWED. LHD

Will was not the world's best reader, but he had stuck at the books until his tenth birthday at the Gullen Creek Methodist School, where he learned enough to get by. Sounding out a couple of the longer words, he repeated the message to Fat Sam. They broke into laughter together. One hundred pounds? It was a crazy amount of money. A good stockman earned that much in a year of round-the-clock labour.

'I've got a better bloody idea,' said Will. 'We won't take this thing to that Joe McCartney cow, wherever the hell Kyungra Station is, but open the damn thing up ourselves. It seems pretty certain to me that whatever's

inside is worth a sight more than a hundred pounds.'
He was already reaching for his knife to cut the package
open when Fat Sam reached out a restraining hand and
touched it on Will's forearm.

'What?' Will asked.

Just then they heard a whoop from towards the sun,
and Jim was running pell-mell towards them.

'Traps,' he cried.

'How many?' Will shouted.

Jim held out his right hand, fingers extended. 'This
many. An' a tracker; pack-horses.'

'Five traps and a tracker,' Will translated aloud, for
Jim had not yet learned the knack of English counting.
'How far away?'

Jim used his hand like a sundial to indicate an angle
of some five or ten degrees. This was intended to show
the movement of the sun over time. Will's translation
was that the police column would be there in twenty or
thirty minutes.

'Damn Clarkie,' spat Fat Sam. 'He brang traps right
to us.'

'No point wallopin' a dead man about it now,' cried
Will. 'Just get the horses, and Jim, you sweep the sign all
around. I'll collect the gear.'

Thinking quickly, Will used his knife to tear away at
Clarkie's saddle-girth, making it look as though it had
torn through, rather than removed by human hands. He

then arranged the saddle just behind the corpse. This done, Will scooped up the canvas-wrapped parcel addressed to the mysterious Joe McCartney and tidied the pannikins and quart pots, one of which he filled with water twice, using it to douse the fire before covering the warm, smoking coals over with earth.

Meanwhile Fat Sam hunted up the plant, and Jim used a leafy branch to sweep their sign away from the dust. Will assisted with tacking up the nags, pushing rifles into scabbards, filling saddlebags and loading and balancing packs by eye.

One of the pack-horses – a baldy-faced little grey gelding, caught sight of some leaves hanging low from an adjacent kurrajong tree, and decided to test their edible qualities. He reared to get at it, taking Will off guard and overbalancing him into the branch. It took a strong heave of the shoulders and arms to drag the animal back out.

Having re-established control Will saw that the others were all but ready to ride out. 'You done there, Jim?'

Jim paused in his labours and shot such a poisonous glare at Will that it required no follow-up with words. The three men were mates – equals. They rode together because they wanted to, but the white man was the only one with a disposition for giving orders. No one liked taking them, and when he overstepped the mark, they let him know.

Soon enough, however, they were swinging up onto the saddle leather, with the horses nervously impatient, fresh from good pasture, rest and water, ready to move on. Jim led the way, and Will took second place, riding with a good natural seat, heels down, and with a deft horseman's touch on the reins. Sam came last, with the packhorses and spares strung behind him. They rode at a fast trot that they could keep up all day, if necessary, with the dramatic outlines of Belougery Spire and Crater Bluff in the distance. This was Warrumbungle country, and no trap could follow if it proved necessary for them to hide.

Jim, as he rode, mimicked the bird calls that came constantly from the trees and surrounding hills, recreating each sound so perfectly that it was indistinguishable from the original. Some calls, such as that of the golden whistler or lorikeet he made with pursed lips. The chatter of a willy wagtail, or a pigeon's coo, came from the whole of his mouth and throat.

This was a pleasure to hear and to be around, and many times in the past Will had whipped around expecting to see a currawong on a perch just behind him, but finding only Jim with a self-satisfied gleam in his eye.

After a while Fat Sam dropped behind. One of the packs – the same baldy-face grey who had caused Will some grief back at the camp – was slowing down the others, seemingly lame in one foot, and Will heard his mate urging the creature on. If it slowed them down too much, Will knew, they would have to unburden the grey and share his load between the others.

Not thirty minutes after their departure, they paused in a pass between two boulder-studded hills for a pull of water and to wait for Sam to catch up. It was only when Will went to hang his waterbag back on a saddle dee that he happened to look down at his jacket. As soon as he saw the torn patch of blue serge, he threw back his head and swore. 'Oh, damn and blast me for a careless fool.'

'All true,' said Fat Sam, reining in beside him. 'But why you say it now?'

Jim found this statement humorous, and he threw back his head and laughed. It was a contagious sound – Sam had once said that when Jim laughed, even the echoes of his laughter laughed along with him – but Will was in no mood for amusement.

He held the torn material where the button used to be between his thumb and forefinger. 'I've lost a button, see?'

'When you lose it?'

'I dunno.' Will turned to Jim. 'Did ya see a button back there on the ground at all?'

Jim ceased his whistling. 'If it were there, I would'a

seen it, bloke.'

'Maybe when that darned grey tried a bolt on me. I did feel somefink catch on the branch.' His horse made a determined attempt to drop his head and Will reefed it up. 'This is serious – everyone for a hundred miles knows that blasted jacket, and if they find the button the traps will be after us in a minute. I'll have to go back and take a gander – see if I spot it before they do. Once they find Clarkie's body they'll 'ave to bury 'im or take 'im to town, so that might give me the chance I need.'

Fat Sam nodded his head in agreement. 'Most likely they bury him.'

'That's what I reckon. So, if I lost that button when the grey reared, I might be able to creep in and find it.'

Gamilaroi Jim shook his head and spat to one side. He never wore a shirt at all, winter or summer, and could not understand Will's practice of sporting a fancy jacket for no reason at all. 'A spring gully-raker makes lesser noise than you when you are creepin', bloke. Clever thing to do is ride away and hope the traps are blind like you.'

Will bristled, his pride hurt. 'I'll have you know that I can creep like a damn brown snake when I have to. Anyway, I'm heading back for a gander. If it aren't a goer, I'll give it up. I think we should get some distance away though. How about we meet at the Fig Tree camp tonight?'

'Righti-oh,' said Fat Sam, but then he inclined his head at Will's saddle bag, where the canvas-wrapped parcel he had taken from Clarkie's corpse made a bulge in the leather. 'You should leave package. Case you get lagged.'

Will pulled a face, 'An' let you two barsteds open it and run like goannas with the insides? Fat chance.'

Sam's face showed no emotion: he just shrugged his shoulders. 'Jim an' me will be at the Fig Tree camp, but ...' he stopped and waggled his finger, 'don't bring police when you come.'

Will rolled his eyes, 'Don't treat me like a new-chum. An' youse better sort out that lame horse or you'll never get anywhere.'

Satisfied that he had the upper hand in the argument, Will turned his horse, and with a light stab of his heels, headed back the way they had come.

2

AS HE RODE back towards their river camp, Will reflected on how the three of them had met. It was one of those things that fate carelessly allows, like three dry, windswept leaves blowing into each other's path for no real reason at all.

Five years earlier, Will joined a yard-building team, working at Coomara Station on the Upper Macleay, crafting four-rail panels with morticed joins, all split from white mahogany trunks, and shaped with adze and axe.

It was back-breaking labour, day-in, day-out, and one afternoon in the second week, during a dinner break, the three men had shared the shade of a she-oak tree, eating their damper with corned beef, and drinking mugs of tea.

Not far away, a wagonette arrived, and the manager, the owner, and the owner's two sons were soon seated at a trestle table, with the station cook serving them.

'Bloody toffs,' spat Fat Sam, his own hands roughened with calluses from hard work.

But it was Gamilaroi Jim who pointed towards the station horse paddock, visible from their make-shift chairs of stumps and roots. 'Hey, listen, bloke. I can see a big mob of fillies and colts in there with no brand on 'em. Worth a few bob if anyone had gall enough to make off with 'em.'

Will grinned. 'That's the best idea I've heard in a long time. Count me in.'

Both men turned their eyes to the third. Sam simply inclined his head and raised a calloused thumb.

★ ★ ★ ★ ★

They waited until two nights after the new moon, when there was just enough light to see. Will, Sam and Jim mustered up those young horses and strung them away without raising any alarm from the homestead or men's quarters. The Macleay was low over its pebbled bed, and they rode the first few miles in the shallows, then used scarcely known tracks up to George's Creek, tackling the rugged Eastern Fall, with Gamilaroi Jim sweeping their sign from the path as they went. Reaching Armidale, they swung north, finally crossing the Queensland border near Dirranbandi.

At the town of St George, they made a tidy parcel of cash selling the horses. Will bought a new saddle, moleskins and a rifle. Fat Sam's share disappeared into his purse and stayed there, for he was no gambler like many of his kind. Gamilaroi Jim's takings just seemed to disappear, as they always did. He didn't care too much for money, in any case.

The three of them had ridden together ever since, through thick and thin, thriving on each other's differences and energy. They loved horses, freedom, and the overriding tenet that the property of rich men was fair game.

Now, as Will approached the river clearing, he tied his horse to the lower branch of a boree wattle, leaving the saddle on but loosening the girth for comfort. Also, to assist in silent movement, he removed his spurs and placed them in the saddle bag — this pair tended to tinkle like tiny bells. Despite these preparations he had no intention of spending more than a few minutes on this excursion.

Jim's crack about Will's inability to move silently in the bush was like comparing a hunting python to a dingo. The latter was a clever stalker, but the former was a silent terror. Will could move without sound on almost any landscape, and meld into a tree trunk or rock as if he wasn't there. Jim's ability, however, was magical. He was able to flow like water, weather like stone, or blow like sand from a drift.

Having spotted a low-rise Will dropped to his hands and knees and moved those last few yards in that position. He then popped his head just far enough up that his eyes could scan the scene.

Much had changed since they had ridden away. Two or three policemen were gathered around the body of John Clarke, another was watering horses, and a lone tracker was casting around the area, away from the camp itself.

The man standing over the body was all too recognisable. It was Long Douglas, the sergeant from Coonabarabran. Will smirked to himself at seeing the man, for they'd had more than a few run-ins over the years, most recently over a series of warrants for possession of a stolen horse.

It was not great height that had won Long Douglas his nickname, but the opposite. He was a short little roly-poly bloke — scarcely five feet in his socks, and a little more in his blucher boots with their built-up heels.

Right now, his face was red with anger, and he was throwing orders around the clearing like an angler casting flies. Will's attention had moved on, however, to that little patch of brush where the packhorse had reared, and he had most likely lost his button. His chances, it seemed, of creeping up and scouting around for the missing item without being seen, at least before nightfall, seemed dim. And if Fat Sam was right and they would bury the dead man on the spot, they hadn't picked up a shovel to do so yet.

One of the policemen walked away from the body and was poking around the fringes of the clearing. Jim had done a good job of sweeping away tracks, but with limited time, Will knew, it was hard to disguise the fact that the dusty area around the camp had been swept by *something*.

It occurred to Will that returning to look for the button was a bad idea. The policeman he didn't know was walking around with his head low, in random patterns, and sooner or later he would surely find the button. To make matters worse, the tracker was circling back around the camp, behind Will's position, and letting the traps find his horse was much worse than the discovery of one little button.

For a minute or two Will lay prone, with his fists clenched, knowing that not even Jim would have been able to get to the kurrajong and look around for the button before they noticed him. Will was buggered, snookered and helpless. What could he do but withdraw and hurry back to the others?

Just then he heard a startled whinny from behind. His horse. The tracker must have cast further out and seen it. He jumped to his feet and ran pell-mell for the spot.

Long Douglas spotted the running man straight away and a quick glance revealed to Will that the policeman was working at the buckle of his holster.

Ahead the tracker had almost reached Will's horse but backed off in surprise as that individual bore down on him.

The man was not armed and had no wish to tangle with the swiftly moving and now agitated Will. Reaching the horse, despite the urgency, Will took the time to tighten the girth, untie the reins, slip the toe of his boot into the stirrup and mount cleanly.

The whipcrack of a bullet passed not an inch from his ear, seeming to suck the air away from inside his skull, but by then his heels had dug sharply into his mount's flanks, and the animal's own natural awareness of the situation caused him to drive powerfully off his hind legs and into a gallop.

Two more shots boomed out into the stillness of the afternoon, but Will did not hear the bullets fly, only the sound of discharge and the cries of cockatoos taking wing from the red gums along the creek.

From the next rise, and well out of range Will took a pull to study the scene. With the police horses all in the process of being watered, not one man had so far managed to saddle a horse, and Long Douglas was red-faced and shouting, his voice carrying like a Staffordshire terrier's bark across the scrub.

With a surge of bloody-minded rage Will turned his horse to face the police, 'Come and get me you murdering barsteds,' he shouted. 'Try your hardest anyhow.'

Will knew that his shouted words would rile them up, but he was prepared to back himself. The gelding he rode had bloodlines that, had the owner been an honest man, might have seen him racing at Flemington or Rosehill.

In addition to the usual gaits, this gelding had the ability to slip into a wonderously smooth three-quarter pace, in which one foot always touched the ground – almost as fast as a gallop but much easier on both horse and rider.

It was into this most pleasant state that Will urged his gelding, and as the miles began to pass it occurred to him that now that they were giving chase, the traps would probably never find the lost button after all.

3

THE WESTERN foothills of the Warrumbungle range rise in tangled shafts of stone from the plains, vegetated with a heavy scrub of wattle and gum trees that was hard going for horsemen. Even the grasses were sharp tussocks and spear-grass. Will knew these stone fastnesses well, and later, as he reduced his mount to a trot, he planned his route with care, knowing that Long Douglas was now on his trail.

He anti-tracked as he went, sloshing through creeks, and joining the trails of other travellers or riding amongst herds of sheep or cattle where he sighted them.

Finally, however, he paused on the edge of a place where stone replaced soil on the ground, a flat sheet of sandstone that extended as far as a man can see, studded with bushes, patches of grass and piled-up boulders. There he climbed down from his mount, and using shoe pullers he removed his horse's shoes, for iron will mark stone to the eyes of a skilled tracker.

This achieved, he rode on, keeping, in general, to the sheet of rock. Sometimes it disappeared under sandy soil, or light scrub. Twice he laid false trails, leaving the stone and heading into the bush a ways, before riding back and continuing on. When finally he left the area, a little past sunset, he was confident that he'd left a riddle that should take a tracker a day or two of hard work to decipher.

From there he rode more or less directly to the Brambie Road, through Black Hollow, where he re-shod the gelding. His tracks, from this point on, were soon obliterated by wagon and horse traffic along the road.

It was after midnight, and a light dew was moistening the earth and tickling Will's nostrils when he rode within view of the gas lights of the town of Baradine. On the north-eastern side he splashed through the creek of the same name, climbed a spur and headed along a ridge.

Half an hour later he pushed along a narrow trail, with rock so close on both sides that he could have reached out and brushed his knuckles against the mossy surface with both hands. Minutes later he rode into a tight clearing. A campfire cast a glow against a cliff edge, where ferns and orchids grew, and the waters of a soak that made the place such a desirable refuge glistened on the stone surface.

The familiar figures of Fat Sam, and Gamilaroi Jim

were huddled in blankets next to the coals, between the buttress roots of an enormous rusty fig tree.

Will saw to his horse and drank his fill. A loaf of damper waited in the pan, and he sat alone, eating hungrily. When he had finished, he collected his bedroll from where it had been stowed.

Fat Sam opened one eye, then removed a hand from under the blanket. Between thumb and forefinger, he held a brass button – it was slightly misshapen and somewhat dirty.

Will spat his mouthful on the ground, then leaned forward to examine the item. 'That's my missing button. Where did you find it?'

'Lame grey pack-horse,' said Sam. 'Button caught in between shoe and frog. Not lame no more.' From Jim's swag came the sound of subdued but shaking laughter.

It took Will a minute or two to figure out what must have happened – the horse that half-dragged him into the bushes must have brought his hoof down on the button where it became wedged – a million to one chance – ridiculous, really.

'Shut up, you two. It's not funny, what a blasted waste of time, and that cursed Long Douglas saw me. He might as well have found the damned button.'

Full of infuriated pride Will threw a few sticks on the fire to provide some light, then cleaned the button in a pint-pot of water. With a needle and cotton thread he sewed the button back on, tugging at it fiercely to ensure that it would not part ways again.

This done, finally, fatigued and annoyed at himself, he slithered under the single blanket and made his final preparations for sleep. The last act of this routine never varied. Will dug into a compact leather compendium that stayed in his own saddlebag. From inside he removed a ragged daguerreotype.

The image on the face of that sheet was of a young woman. Eighteen or nineteen years in age, she had long hair, tied into a single flowing stream down to her waist. Her eyes were placid but alert, her chin strong. Underneath was a single word, written in ink: *Helen*.

Will stared at the image. He had loved that girl ever since he had seen the image for sale in a hawker's wagon and paid a shilling for it. To him there had never been a human being as perfect as Helen.

Putting the daguerreotype carefully back in its place, he lay down on his bedroll, pulled the grimy blanket up to his chin, and dreamed.

★ ★ ★ ★ ★

When Will woke up, a little after dawn, he had a lot to think about. In the beauty of that hidden glade the events of the previous day made no sense – a man riding into camp and dropping dead, then a lost button that somehow managed to get wedged into a horse's foot, not to mention a package worth a hundred pounds to the delivery man.

After a breakfast of johnny-cakes and a little cold bacon, Will fetched the canvas package, along with his belt knife, and sat beside the hearth re-reading the message, again wondering who Joe McCartney might be and what must be in the package to be worth one hundred pounds.

'You goin' to open it?' asked Fat Sam.

'I think I might.'

Sam watched, and even Jim was interested enough to break off plaiting some greenhide and come across to watch.

'Where is this Kyungra Station, anyway, bloke?' Jim asked.

Sam crossed his arms in front of his chest and pressed his lips together thoughtfully. 'Up Queensland,' he said. 'Long way west.'

'So, it's a big run then,' said Will. 'Might be a rich barsted owns the place?'

Sam shrugged, unwilling to commit himself on that score. 'I never been there.'

'Darn it all,' said Will. 'I'm just gonna open the blessed thing.'

Before he had a chance to pierce the canvas, however, there was a soft sound from down the hidden track that led to the camp. It was the soft and repetitive oom-oom-oom-oom of the tawny frogmouth, but a little more strident. It was a signal – someone was coming – a friend not an enemy.

Even so, the three men took precautions, fetching carbines or short arms to hand. Will fitted the butt of his Snider to his shoulder, feeling the first hard resistance of the hammer-spring with his thumb. He was not alarmed enough to fully cock it.

The figure that came riding in a moment later was instantly familiar. It was a woman in her early twenties, riding astride in moleskin trousers. Swinging easily off her mount she showed herself to be of medium height, her curly hair hanging loose from the back of a broad-brimmed felt hat. Behind her trailed a single packhorse loaded down with fat canvas packs.

Will hurried to take the newcomer's mount by the bridle while she dismounted. 'No one behind you?' he asked.

'Nah, but you've got trouble,' said the young woman.

He had already moved to embrace her, a clasp that finished with an exchange of pecks on cheeks. The smell of her was more leather and livestock than perfume and flowers.

Elaine Phillips was Will's younger sister by five years, married to a well-to-do cocky just out of Baradine.

'Big trouble,' she breathed. 'The traps surrounded the homestead at dawn this morning ...'

'What in tarnation?' spat Will, but she had not finished.

'They banged on the doors and called us out. I was in my darn nightclothes – the buggers.' She paused. 'They was looking for you.' She looked near to busting into tears. 'Dear God, Will, there's a price on yer head and you're wanted for murder.'

'Murder?' asked Will, mouth open like a cave. 'Murderin' who?'

'Some man they found dead down west of Burbie Canyon.'

Gamilaroi Jim cleared his throat. 'They've pinned you for Clarkie's murder, bloke.'

The blood had drained from Will's face. 'But it was them, what must've done it. They shot him. He fell off of his 'orse like a damn dead crow from its perch, right in front of our eyes.'

'Looking for button was bad idea,' said Fat Sam.

'You're telling me,' said Will, but he turned back to his sister. 'Tell me Lainey, which traps were there. Was it Long Douglas?'

'No. Not him, but they was police from Coona. I recognised one or two. They searched the sheds, even the damned chook house.'

Will shook his head sadly, 'Please don't swear

Lainey, you know Ma would ...'

'You're wanted for bloody murder and yer tellin' me not to swear. Take hold of yourself. You have to work out what to do.'

'You could hand yerself in an' tell the truth,' said Sam.

'Sure, and they'll believe me, won't they? They'll have five bloody police troopers testifyin' that they saw me ride away from the scene of the so-called crime. Besides ... Long Douglas knows he's bangin' me up. He and 'is men shot Clarkie and are pinnin' it on me. God knows what other evidence they've planted to make sure it sticks.' He turned to Sam, 'Are you an' Jim willin' to ride in with me to back up my story?' He gave them a second or two to answer before rattling on, 'No? I didn't think so, because they'll peg you as accessories, not to mention the outstanding warrants they've got on us.'

'We gonna scarper, then bloke?' Jim said.

Will scratched his chin thoughtfully. 'Scarper aren't a word I like to use. Scarperin' is what wallabies, an' bandicoots do. We aren't the types of men to scarper ... but ... it so happens that ...' he looked across at the canvas-wrapped package he had left beside the campfire on a ficus root, 'I have a package to deliver to Kyungra Station up in Queensland. What do you say gentlemen? Do you wish to accompany me on a mission, taking up the noble art of the mail man? We will collect one hundred pounds for our trouble and assess our options from there?'

Sam inclined his head, 'Sounds like best chance.'

'I'm in,' said Jim.

'I'm not letting you buggers skive off and have all the fun,' said Lainey. 'I'm comin' too.'

Will shook his head, 'No ya aren't. You've got an 'usband who looks after ya. I'd 'ave thought you'd have a brat on the way by now.'

Lainey's arms flew to her hips, and angry red blotches appeared on her cheeks. 'Maybe I would if me 'usband weren't shootin' powder an' no shot. An' if marryin' a good church-goin' man for money weren't the dullest thing I ever done. I'm bored out of my head – sittin' down for fancy dinners every night, warmin' church pews every Sunday and with nothin' to do but tell servants what to do. Now 'e wants me to turn you in an' I aren't doin' it. I'm comin' with you.'

Will was too surprised by this speech to respond at first. Finally, however, he made a noise deep in his throat that sounded a bit like a judge considering his verdict.

Lainey followed up her advantage. 'Come on, big brother, you know I won't hold youse up. I'm as good as any fella. I can ride, shoot, an' even throw a punch. I'll tail the horses for youse better than anyone, and you know it to be true and God be my witness.'

'Alrighty,' agreed Will. 'You can come, and since you're all set to go, we'll strike camp ourselves and leave within an hour.'

'What's the plan?' asked Lainey. 'You know you'll have to lead the police trackers on a merry dance to get away scot-free.'

'I only got one plan: it's called the Pillaga,' said Will. 'No man alive can follow us in there and come out still on our trail.'

4

THE PILLIGA scrub was a legend to stockmen and travellers no less than the far-away Murranji, Gulf or Birdsville Tracks. Northward of the Warrumbungles, from Coonabarabran almost as far as Wee Waa, the Pillaga was more than a thousand square miles of semi-arid forest, parts of it so thick that a man could scarcely walk between tree trunks. Losing all perspective of the outside world, more than a few men had wandered deeper and deeper in until they died.

Drovers avoided the place, for it was impossible to keep control of a herd in the trees, and horses disliked the sharp grasses and sandstone ground. There were secret places too – cavernous overhangs and verdant gullies – it was often said that a lifetime could be spent in exploring the Pillaga.

The first evening, after a full day spent following a bridle track through the timber, Jim led them along the edge of a sandstone scarp, to a rock hole holding water beside a fine sweep of sand on which to throw their swags. There were signs that some of Jim's people had been there in recent times, for there were bare footprints in the damp sand near the edges, and scorched wallaby bones near the charred remnants of a campfire.

That night, while they risked a fire with flames leaping high to illuminate the camp, Lainey entertained the men with stories of the various characters in and around Baradine. Fat Sam continued his recent interest in teaching Jim how to read and write Chinese characters — an activity Will regarded as completely useless – and who spent his own time finishing off the green-hide harness he'd been making, off and on, for a few weeks.

They retired early, to the tune of the crickets, frogs and the crackle of coals in the fireplace. Ten or fifteen minutes later, however, Lainey called out from her bedroll. 'Stop yer rustlin', whoever that is. There's a lady in camp.' A guilty silence followed.

'It's comin' from Will's swag,' said Jim.

'Pah! So, I've got an itch,' cried Will. 'You'd think a fella would be able to scratch a damned itch without people humbuggin' him.'

'You've had the same itch since you was twelve an' a half,' said Lainey, 'an' if you'd stop lookin' at that damned picture of that girl ...'

'I told you not to swear,' said Will.

'Ah, just go to sleep,' she said. And the rustling stopped.

★ ★ ★ ★ ★

The next morning, they reached a thickly forested waterway called Etoo Creek, where they dismounted for a bogey and saw to the horses. From here on, though they had to take care, for sections of the valley were being cleared by men with axes, crosscut saws and teams of bullocks. They passed close to several tree-cutters' camps, and even a sawmill that hadn't been there a few months earlier.

'Darned progress,' said Will. 'I wish they'd leave the bush alone. Those rich barsteds in Sydney are behind it — this country is just a money-making machine for them.'

These incursions, however, were easy enough to skirt, and most of the time the four of them travelled well. Jim and Sam teased Will so mercilessly about the lost button and mysterious night noises that for a time he rode ahead and alone, before he weakened and dropped back.

By late on that second afternoon, they had switched a little to the east, leaving all signs of civilisation behind, and onto a track so narrow they dismounted and led the horses through, stopping a couple of times to let thick black or brown snakes glide regally away. There was something about the place that quietened them. The teasing stopped, and even Lainey was struck silent by the closed-in forest.

Jim was leading the way then, and Will's mind wandering, when his mate stopped abruptly, rigid as a pole, raising a hand in a signal for them to cease walking, then cupping it to his ear.

Will, hearing nothing, waited, watching while Jim handed his reins to Sam, then dug in his saddle bags for the iron hatchet he always carried. This was one of the few implements Jim owned. It had an iron head of unknown pedigree, greatly curved from eye to heel, and kept so sharp that he used it interchangeably with a knife.

It was also Jim's favoured weapon, and at the sight of it in his mate's right hand, Will silently slid his Snider from its sheath. He flicked the lever down to load up a round from the box in his saddlebags, easing the huge blunt cartridge into the chamber so that it did not make so much as a click.

Lainey came up to whisper in his ear. 'What's happening?'

Will's shrug was his only reply, for his eyes were still on Jim, who had moved away into the trees some ten paces. Then, with a bound, still holding the hatchet in his hand, he began to climb.

At first Will thought that Jim might be trying to observe some enemy up ahead, but then, reaching a branch on which he sat, Jim took up the hatchet and began to attack a hollow branch alongside. In ten or twenty strokes the branch fell to the ground and Jim shimmied back down.

'Sugar bag,' he smiled, and kneeled to hack at the branch that now lay at his feet, ignoring a squadron of stingless native bees that swarmed from the site.

Will unloaded his weapon and replaced it in the scabbard, walking up to see Jim already delving with his hands into the waxy hive, his fingers coated with honey. It was the Gamilaroi man's favourite food.

'You frightened the living daylights out of me,' said Will. 'Why all the carrying on?'

Jim pointed with one honeyed finger at his ear, 'I need to listen bloke. Heard the bees in their hives. Can't do that with you making noise.'

'Orright then,' said Will. 'You gonna share that honey or what?'

★ ★ ★ ★ ★

The next day they made a slow twenty miles, and still the Pilliga scrub went on. Lainey, who had been only in the outer forest in the past, was dumbstruck by the extent of it.

'I just wish that I could see full daylight again,' she said. 'Feels like bloody ages since I did.'

'Swearin' won't help,' said Will. 'I told you before.'

Lainey made a face, 'Here's a deal. You stop swearin' and I'll stop swearin'. Right?'

Will said nothing. It didn't seem like a fair bargain to him.

The plan was not to go into camp that evening, but to exit the forest in darkness, and travel as far away as possible in the night. Yet, with some ten miles still to go they risked joining a new timber-getters track that ran along a creek called the Coghill.

After all, they had not seen a sign of traps since their flight began, and they were many miles away from Baradine. In fact, it was easy to forget that Will had an accusation of murder hanging over him.

The carefree nature of their escape was about to change.

5

OLD WEDGE-TAILED eagle, perched on a crag on a peak to the south, had seen many things over the years. From vast heights and giddy perches, he had seen the white people consolidate their domains.

There had been whites in the fertile plains and valleys besides the mountains all his life, but much had happened in the last decade. More fences, more building, more cattle and sheep. More barking dogs and roads.

The eagle was a huge bird, with a wingspan of eight feet. On the ground he stood nearly four feet tall, and his talons were hooked and curved like an Afghan's knife.

Hungry again and knowing that he had to take advantage of the afternoon thermals before evening cooled the air, the eagle left his stony perch with a stately movement of his wings. Then, floating high above the ground he scanned with eyes that can discern eight times more detail than a human eye.

Though he rarely felt threatened by their kind, he kept himself aware of the movement of men, both afoot and on horseback, those who tilled soil and those who formed ranks. He did not like their noise and their guns, but he watched them, nonetheless.

Over the past three days he had seen a drama play out through and around his domain. He was very familiar with the dark-skinned people of his lands. Their relationship was long-standing, the result of uncountable generations passing, sharing the plains, mountains and rivers.

The eagle had seen the dead white rider fall from the horse. Then, out of interest, observed the three men, one of whom had been familiar to him all his life – born on the banks of the Teridgerie, and washed in those brown waters on the day of his birth. The three men had ridden away from the dead man. He had seen them separate. Then the troop of riders with rifles slung on their backs ride in.

He had seen the three ride into the Pilliga, with a woman now in their company. Today he had seen something else as well. A small patrol of mounted and uniformed gun-carriers had entered the forest from the northern end and set up camp.

From his elevated eye the wedge-tailed eagle saw the three, including the young man he had known ever since he was a fledgling, riding towards a trap.

Very close, probably too late, but the wedge-tailed eagle altered the angle of his wings and descended. From a thousand metres to one hundred, just over the three men.

He emitted a single cry, and he saw the black man look up. The message had been understood. The wedge-tailed eagle flapped his wings and soared away.

★ ★ ★ ★ ★

Will was in the lead, his mind on other things. It was perhaps an hour from sundown, but already quite dull in the forest. He saw the eagle but did not understand its message.

Jim barked a warning. 'Watch out. Trouble ahead.'

Will did not have time to check his advance, but at least he was fully alert when a clearing loomed, and he registered the sight of men and horses in residence there.

The men wore the dark woollen blazers and kepi hats of the New South Wales Mounted Police. One was leaning over a cooking fire, another unsaddling a horse and a third and fourth were in the process of pitching a tent. Four rifles leaned together in one of those ridiculous, to Will's mind, pyramids of guns that make it impossible to take one without toppling the others but look aesthetically pleasing to the eyes of inexperienced men.

It was too late to turn back easily. Jim and the others were pressing close behind. The policemen had seen the incoming horsemen yet appeared to be immobile with shock in those first moments before they collected their wits. Taking these factors into account, Will made the giddying but instant decision to ride on through the camp.

'Yah,' he cried, as much to encourage those behind him as to urge on his gelding. The prick of the spur did the rest. His mount overcame its instinct to turn from the unfamiliar scene and dropped his head and surged into a gallop.

The troopers ran like bandicoots for their rifles, and one, wearing a corporal's chevrons, managed to strip his squirt from a holster. The first shot came as Will made it through the clearing, steering his mount into the continuation of the narrow track. The sound did nothing to slow his horse's pace, and it galloped on.

Then, when it seemed that the danger had passed, scarcely a hundred paces past, he heard Jim's cry from behind him. 'Hold up there. Lainey's down.'

Will's mount was desperate to run, but his rider had trained him for a one-rein stop, and it was this manoeuvre he used now to bring the gelding back to a walk. This achieved, Will turned him sharply with knee and rein to face the others. Sam had picked up the reins of Lainey's still-bucking horse but was struggling to control both that animal and the string of packs and spares.

'Was Lainey shot?' Will asked.

'Dunno, maybe shot, maybe thrown,' Sam said, his voice sounding as close to rattled as Will had ever heard him.

'Darn it,' said Will, dismounting smoothly and fastening his horse to the nearest tree. 'Hey Jim, come back with me, while the barsteds are still rattled.' The Gamilaroi man moved to tether his own mount, and both men released and loaded their firearms.

Even as he loped back down the track, Will heard the comforting sound of Jim's feet behind him. He felt not the faintest touch of fear in his heart, only terrible resolve. Family was sacrosanct. Family was everything.

I should have backed off, he berated himself. *I shouldn't have charged through an armed camp like that.*

Ahead he could see Lainey laid out on the dust, with her left arm spread and her other scrunched awkwardly beneath her body. One side of her face was smeared with dirt from the track, and she had claw-like lines of blood on her cheek.

The trap corporal was in the act of bending over to check on her, still holding his revolver. The other three policemen had just reached their stockpile of weapons and were shouldering arms as Will and Jim reached the clearing and stopped, carbines aimed from the hip at the troopers. Will saw now how young they were.

'Is she dead?' roared Will at the corporal. 'Have you kilt my sister, you mongrel dogs?'

The corporal swivelled his revolver to cover them. 'Give up, an' drop yer weapons. It's four against two. We'll blow holes in both of you before you can shoot.'

'You drop 'em,' Will returned.

'If you're still holding those rifles at the count of three,' said the corporal, raising the revolver and sighting along the barrel, 'my men and I will shoot.'

Will knew the odds. Even if he and Jim shot a man each, the other two would kill them long before they could reload their single-shot weapons. Worse, one of the traps had a Henry repeating rifle and the corporal had a six-shot revolver. Despite those practicalities, Will had no desire to become a police-killer, not even with Lainey lying there, God only knew how badly injured.

'One,' said, the corporal, 'two ...'

The next thing that happened surprised every man in that clearing. Lainey, who had appeared to be dead, or at least as good as, lifted her knees, uncoiled her body and moved with the grace of a water rat into a crouch.

With a lightning-fast right hand she snatched the heavy revolver from the corporal's hand, somehow backed up into a standing position and covered him, switching the weapon from hand to hand nervously as if anxious to use it.

'Three guns against three now,' cried Lainey. 'An' if I'm not mistaken that's our other mate just coming down the track with 'is carbine.'

Will whipped his head around to look, seeing that Fat Sam was indeed ambling down the track towards them, seemingly in no hurry, but of course he'd had to secure the horses before coming back to help.'

'That's four guns against three,' Lainey continued.

Will shot her a grin. He'd never been so happy to hear the sound of her voice in his life. He took over from her neatly. 'Drop those weapons, lads. And do it quick 'cause I ain't in a good mood.'

Nothing happened at first, but with an instinct for pressing home an advantage, Will fired a round from the Snider not a yard from their feet. The Snider is a fearsome weapon, originally a British Army issue muzzle loader, converted *en masse* to breech weapons and sold to every outback pioneer on a budget.

Both rifle and carbine versions fire a .577 calibre ball with enough powder behind it to blow a mine-face. Now, channelled and contained by the surrounded trees, the boom of discharge was like a minute of thunder distilled to a fraction of a second. Striking the earth, the ball scooped up a grave-hole's worth of dirt, threw it against the troopers, and left a gout of black gun smoke hanging in the air.

Will had a new cartridge sliding into the chamber in an instant. The prospect of facing another detonation was too much for the troopers, who turned tail and ran back down the track deeper into the scrub. Only one man dropped his rifle, but the others did not try to use theirs, being pursued by all three men at first, until Will broke off the chase and let Jim and Sam continue on, while he went back to Lainey.

'You're alive,' he said wonderingly. I thought you was shot.'

'Of course, I'm alive,' she cried. 'My bloody horse shied when that trap barsted started shootin'. I've got a hell of a headache, though.' Will held her hand so tight that she complained, 'Hey, I got enough aches and pains without you breakin' me fingers.'

Jim and Sam returned, and the former hefted the dropped Henry rifle. 'I always wanted one of these,' he said, breaking open the action and examining the chamber. 'It's the old rimfire one, but if I can find enough ammo it'll be good fun on the track.'

'And it looks like Lainey got herself a squirt,' smiled Will. 'Police-issue Webley too.'

Lainey grinned back and raised the barrel to the sky. 'An' I ain't afraid to use it, so watch out you buggers.'

6

WILL WAS aware that two of the traps still had their rifles, and that soon the patrol would gather the pluck to wander back. It would be easy enough to find a good lie and start shooting, and he doubted that the policemen would hold back after being outfoxed and humiliated.

Time was therefore of the essence, and while Jim gathered what ammunition he could find for his new rifle, and Sam substituted the best of the police horses for the worst of theirs, Will also examined the traps' camp kit, souveniring a few un-chipped mugs and some good woollen blankets.

Then, with Lainey riding in the middle of the file with Jim, they set off into the fading dusk, still following the creek. Will was aware now that rather than having made a sneaky move through the Pilliga to an unknown exit, they had committed what the police would view as a serious crime.

Will knew how easily a shot fired at the ground became "attempted murder" and how a group of police always saw the exact same thing, even when events hadn't quite gone down the way they said.

There would, he knew for a fact, soon be a very determined force on their trail. 'Speed now,' he cried. 'We need to put some miles between us and them.'

They were soon mounted up and moving, slowing down as a mauve and yellow dusk darkened the forest. As night fell, however, Will began to wonder at his wisdom in riding through the Pilliga forest in the first place. He started to wonder when it would ever end. For the sake of speed, they followed the track as they found it, and at any time they might have stumbled on another patrol or even a main force.

On a quick stop he changed mounts to a night horse, a bay mare. Jim took a chance on one of the better police horses, while Sam stuck with the clumper he favoured for its strength and endurance. They carried on to the north, still following Coghill Creek, on station land now, cleared in places, and they used the riverine scrub as cover, riding along sheep trails, tufts of wool shining in the moonlight on trees on either side.

'It'll take those useless buggers back there all night to ride for help, so we've got a bit of time at least,' said Will.

'Maybe,' said Sam. 'Telegraph station at Cuttabri. Maybe they ride there. Three, four hours.'

'That's true, but even so, let's hole up and get a bit of shut-eye.' He was aware that Lainey was struggling with the pace of their flight, admitting to feeling a little crook in the head from when she'd hit the ground.

'I feel like I ain't slept for a week,' she said. And after they had eaten, they seeped into their swags like puddles of water, with each of the men on watch in turn, while the others snored softly.

★ ★ ★ ★ ★

Awake before dawn, they continued on the journey, crossing the busy Pillaga Road beside a bridge made of tree trunks laid with sleepers, waiting in the scrub nearby while Jim swept their sign from the track.

'Hey bloke,' Jim called out. 'Some riders comin' fast. Want me to ask them what's goin' on?'

'Good idea,' Will called back, then turned to Fat Sam. 'Would you take the horses down the gully a ways?'

Sam looked back at him levelly. 'Why not *you* take horses down the gully a ways?'

'Listen mate,' said Will. 'Jim's about to parley with some men on the road — I need to keep an ear out for what's goin' on.'

'Bossy mongrel,' spat Sam.

Lainey stood up. 'Come on Sam, I'll give you a hand.'

Sam shrugged and went with Lainey, while Will turned his attention to the road, where Jim was undergoing a transformation that he had seen once or twice before.

One moment Gamilaroi Jim was a young, athletic rascal with a swagger and more cheek than a willy wagtail. As Will watched, his head went down, his eyes fell to the ground, respectful and humble. His lack of a shirt had a few moments ago seemed like bravado, now it was poverty. The taut muscles of his belly now made him look half-starved rather than fit and strong.

At the same time Will watched the horsemen ride in, and when they reached the bridge Jim was calling out, 'A penny! This-fella beg you for a penny for some tucker to eat.'

The riders reined in, and the leading man, a stout fellow with a bristle moustache, laughed and reached into his pocket. 'Here's yer penny boy, now don't spend it on strong drink.' He threw the coin and it fell at Jim's feet, jangling and spinning.

'Gawd bless you mista, thank you bery much.'

Another one of the group walked his horse closer to Jim, then removed his felt hat and used the brim to wipe sweat from his forehead. 'Hey boy, you 'aven't seen a gang of armed ruffians passing through 'ave you?'

'What they look like mista?'

The rider pulled a sheet of paper from an inside pocket and unrolled it. 'This man is the leader. His name's Will Jones, a murderer no less, and there's a reward of five hundred pounds for 'is apprehension. We work on Cuttabri Station yonder, and the boss has sent us all out to 'elp look for the bastard, figuring that 'e'll pass through this way.'

'I hain't seen 'im mista. But he's a cruel seemin' man to me. Very cruel — ugly man. Disgustin' thievin' …'

From his hiding place in the bushes Will hissed under his breath. It was just like Jim to start having fun with what was a possibly dangerous situation.

'Well, I'll tell you what,' said the moustached one, 'we're riding down as far as Barkers Creek to look for tracks and be back this way in two hours. If you stay right 'ere and watch the road, I'll give you another penny when we come back, orright?'

One of the men, who had been silent to that point, wore a cabbage-tree hat and dark-stained dungarees, spoke for the first time. 'I wouldn't trust this boy as far as I would kick 'im. Doesn't Will Jones ride with a black man and a celestial?'

'I've heard he does,' the moustached man said, then leaned down from his horse towards Jim. 'You don't know this Will Jones, do you?'

Jim shook his head, 'Never seen him. Never at all. I don't go alonga bad men like that.'

'Well alright. But you stay right here, and we'll be back.'

The horsemen urged their horses on, and Jim kept up the pretence until they were long gone, at which point he crossed the road and walked, still grinning, towards Will.

'Did you have to make a complete cow of yourself?' asked Will. 'Now they'll come back in a couple of hours and expect you to be there waiting for them. They might look around for tracks because you're not there. And who gave you the right to call me ugly?'

Still bantering about the exchange, the pair walked down the sheep-trail to re-join Lainey and Sam, who had found a shady patch to wait, quite unperturbed.

'Bad news,' said Will. 'After yesterday evenin's caper the traps've put five hundred pounds on my head and sounds like every man with a horse and a rifle is out looking for me.'

'Police must be bonkers,' said Sam. 'You not worth half that much money.' He scratched his chin seriously. 'But since you never done that murder, maybe like I said, the best thing is for you to turn yourself in — they got no evidence that you killed Clarkie. If you keep runnin' it makes you look guilty.'

Will rounded on him. 'I already look guilty, an' you know well enough that lookin' guilty is the same as bein' guilty.'

'That's unfair,' said Lainey. 'But I guess it's true.'

To Will's eyes she looked a little better now, though a grey bruise was now showing on her cheek under the scratches.

'Are you alright?' he asked.

''Course I am. Nothing to complain about.'

'Must've been a good knock to the 'ead.'

'Knock some sense into me,' she smiled.

Will rummaged in his saddle bag for a tin flask with a little rum in it. 'Here, a bit a' this will help.'

Lainey took a long swig then passed the flask round, and it did seem to Will that her colour improved.

Jim, after drinking down his share, leaned back against a tree and produced a clay pipe with one hand, stuffed the bowl with tobacco and offered the pouch to the others. They were soon all smoking furiously.

'Maybe,' Jim said, 'we could dig out that package you want to deliver in Queensland, open it up and divide whatever loot is inside, then split up. It'll make it harder for them to chase us, bloke.'

'I'm not keepin' anyone with me,' said Will, 'but I'd rather stay together, and to be honest I like the sound of a hundred pounds in cash for nothing more than a long ride, an' being safely across the border in Queensland. If this Kyungra Station is a good one we can maybe get work, lay low for a while, then head further north. I've always wanted to look around up towards the Gulf country.'

'How far to the Namoi, d'ya reckon?' Lainey asked.

'Fifteen mile, no more,' said Will. 'Should be there today even with a cautious ride. I've heard the waters are up, but here's a hand-punt we can get across on if floods hain't carried it away.' He looked at the others. 'If you ride on with me an' we're caught you could get charged as bein' accessories, or even shot if some trigger-happy barsted gets you in 'is sights. If you want to slip off, now's the time to do it.'

No one made a move, and Will spat the taste of tobacco out of his mouth. 'Then let's get to that damned river before sundown and every barsted for a hundred mile is after us.'

7

HAVING LEFT the dense scrub of the Pilliga behind, it was a relief to follow the sheep-pads along the creek. They had to skirt a few out-stations and a couple of selector's cottages, but they saw no one, and Will was growing increasingly confident.

Police reinforcements, Will reasoned, would need to ride from Wee Waa, and stockmen chasing the bounty on his head would, after a day or two, return to their regular employment. Even though he was wanted for murder, John Clarke was an outsider without many friends, and surely his death had caused few tears.

Yet, even after this optimistic assessment had settled into his brain, several things niggled away. The first was that the traps had placed five hundred pounds on his head, which was not a small amount of money. The second was that perhaps there was also some interest in the canvas package in his saddlebags.

These worries paled into significance when, just as they climbed a rounded hill after a long afternoon's ride, with the sun settling redly towards the plains, they were able to look back towards a slight rise in the farmland a mile to the south.

Will watched five horsemen converge with another three, the latter dressed in police garb.

'They seen us,' said Sam.

'I'm not surprised,' said Will, hiding his nervousness. 'There's a lot of you to see.'

'How far to the river now?' asked Lainey.

'Three or four mile,' said Will. 'You can see the line of trees almost swallered up by the haze. We can do it at a gallop — the horses will be blown, but they can recover at the ferry.'

There was no need for further talk. Will's horse dug in and sprang away, with the others in file behind, taking the stony northern side of the hill in their stride, the horses steady performers who enjoyed a run as much as their owners did.

At the foot of the hill they joined a station track that wound around the low ground, and now there was no further need for subterfuge. Riding hell-for-leather for the river was a better option.

At these speeds horses eat up the ground, four miles at a gallop achievable in ten to fifteen minutes. Yet, the packhorses were not so fast, and the string of spares under Sam's care slowed down the group so that after the first exhilarating rush the unencumbered members of the group were constantly backing off to the trot to stay with the group.

'We can't compete with free riders,' said Will. 'We'll be lucky to reach the river before them.'

The last half-mile was the most hair-raising, with the sound of hoofbeats audible from close behind. Finally, however, ahead came the line of trees that guarded the Namoi, and now even the packs seemed to understand that something was behind them that needed to be avoided. Foam flecked the neck of Will's mount, and his flanks were heaving. He knew he'd have to pull up soon or risk overheating him.

Now they were into the river scrub, with the urgent cries of their pursuers in their ears. The river itself appeared before them – brown and wide and flooded with summer rains. It was like standing on the edge of a cliff, for it was an insurmountable barrier — far too wide and deep to swim the horses across.

Will looked for the ferry and saw it a hundred yards upstream, thankfully on their side of the river, a platform of planks mounted on barrels, big enough for a couple of wagons and operated by a hand windlass hauling on hemp ropes that sagged from supports on either bank, running parallel across the stream.

'There,' Will cried, 'hurry.'

And as they rode through that bank mud, dollops of dirt thrown from hooves flew, coating sweating hides, trousers, boots and leggings.

'Stop and surrender in the Queen's name!' came a shout from behind them.

'Not my blasted queen,' muttered Jim as the first gunshot sounded from behind them.

Will glanced back to see that it was a pistol shot, almost impossible to deliver accurately from a moving horse, and no real danger until the police and their posse of stockmen could stop and level their weapons.

They reached the ferry at a run and rushed it in a disorganised mob. The horses were by now more interested in the water than in entering an unfamiliar vehicle and it was necessary to dismount and lead them on to the platform.

Then, when Jim began to turn the winding-wheel it seemed that their weight had settled the ferry into the mud of the bank.

'We'll have to get off again, and push,' said Will. 'Do it, and I'll deter these damn traps and their mates from riding closer.'

Without asking he took the repeating Henry rifle from Jim's scabbard and stepped off the ferry, taking up a good stance and aiming just above the heads of the oncoming horsemen.

He hadn't realised how dark it was getting until he

saw the muzzle flash, and a streak of flame as the recoil told on his shoulder.

The heavy projectile flew close above the pursuers' heads with an accompanying shockwave of sound. Even if this had not deterred the men, it certainly did their horses, for most of them either bucked or tried to turn, and Will worked the lever again. The second shot was not quite as successful, but he glanced behind to see that their own horses were half on, half off the ferry, and that Jim had succeeded in driving it free of the mud. He was now winding furiously while Sam and Lainey attempted to get the remainder of the plant aboard.

Will turned and ran for the vehicle, jumping aboard as it lurched forward into the stream, grabbed by the current so that it moved rapidly out of reach of the one packhorse they were still trying to get on board – the poor old baldy-faced grey.

'Leave him,' Will yelled. 'Get on here yourselves.' He then rested the rifle against one of the vertical poles in the corners of the ferry and sent a round towards the police and stockmen who were now variously charging into the shallows on horseback or dismounting and trying to reach the gear mechanisms that held the ropes at the ends of the ferry.

The shot, followed by another, kept heads down momentarily, giving Sam and Lainey time to consolidate their position on board. The former was still hanging onto a long rope with the final pack horse attached. The poor animal was now almost out of depth, with no way to scramble on board.

'Let it go,' said Will. 'Or we'll drown him with those heavy packs on.'

Sam did so, and they watched the horse swim back towards the shore with half their gear, fortuitously blocking return fire from their pursuers.

'Almost all the food,' lamented Sam.

'You could do with a famine for a day or two,' Will said grimly. 'We'll survive.'

But by then the police party was at work on the ferry gears, attempting to jam the cogs with heavy fallen branches from the river red gums that lined the banks. Others had retrieved their rifles from their scabbards and the first shots rang out. Jim was putting all his strength into the winder, but it was having little or no effect. Their forward progress had stalled, with the current pushing the ferry sideways.

Will knew that they were a sitting target, and sooner or later a police bullet would find its mark.

'Cut, cut,' cried Fat Sam. 'Cut ropes.' And he pointed to the ropes leading to the near bank.

Will acted swiftly, pulling his knife from the sheath at his belt, moving to the corners of the vessel and using the well-honed blade to sever the ropes that held them to the near bank.

'Now,' Fat Sam urged. 'Tie up ropes to other side.'

Fingers manipulating the rough hemp strands, they knotted both ropes to one of the upright beams so that the ferry was still fixed to the northern bank. The flooded Namoi current now had them in its grip, and downstream they went, swinging on a pendulum arc – no longer at the mercy of the gears.

When Will appreciated what was happening, he slapped Fat Sam affectionately on the shoulder. 'Yer a bloody genius. The ferry's taking us across, away from them, without us lifting a finger.' They were also moving very fast, and while a few rifle shots raised geysers on the dark river around them, none came too close.

Scarcely two minutes must have passed before the far bank loomed and the ferry nudged against a muddy shelf. They led the horses out, climbed a steep bank in the darkness with much slipping, swearing and panting, then assembled on the high bank.

'Shame about the pack horse,' said Lainey. And they all agreed. He'd been an unusually spirited animal, and had some quirks they all liked, Besides, almost all their food had been on his back. Still, at least they had their bedrolls and cooking gear; food could be obtained anywhere.

8

THE DAYS that followed were of careful flight, in country that Jim knew like the back of his hand. At Collarenebri they found the Barwon River also flooded. The party managed to walk and swim the horses across at a well-known crossing, but it was unsuitable for wheeled-traffic, and the town was full of stranded travellers, their Cobb and Co coaches lying idle down Earl Street.

On reaching any town, Sam's first preoccupation was to make sure that there were no other Chinese there, and as usual, he observed the place from a hidden nook before even thinking about riding in. In fact, one of Sam's objectives in life was to avoid people of his own race wherever they appeared.

From the little Will knew of the situation his mate, on first reaching Australia, had been a hired lackey, little better than a slave-labourer, on the Margaret River goldfields in the Northern Territory, on which several sections of the Chinese workings were controlled by a Cantonese Tong. The resulting gold was usually shipped back to China. When Sam had apparently hatched a plan to intercept and ride away with one of these shipments he was caught in the act. He managed to escape alive, without the gold and with a Tong price on his head.

Will understood that Sam did not fear Chinese from Peking, easily distinguishable because they wore pigtails, but only those from Canton, who wore their hair in a bun, as Sam did himself.

Once Sam had decided that there was nothing to fear in Collarenebri, it was he who walked in during the late afternoon to case the place – study the two stores and decide on the easiest mark. They were desperate for food, and it was deemed to be cheaper and less risky to take what they wanted rather than buy it.

Sam reported back with a solid plan to remove what they needed from one of the shops, along with news that the front facades of both stores bore posters with Will's face on them, and the word WANTED for MURDER and FIVE HUNDRED POUND REWARD blazoned underneath.

Ironically, one of these posters was pasted just a few feet above the spot where Will and Sam levered a board away. Through this wriggling-space they carried off a wide selection of goods. When it was done, they replaced the board, leaving no sign that they had been there apart from a missing sack of flour, a bag of salt, some tea, tobacco and condiments.

'A true thief is an artist,' Will lectured his mates around the campfire, still flushed with the success of the enterprise. 'He steals only from those who can afford it and leaves little sign of his passing.'

Fat Sam, tired of the monologue, went and ate his johnny-cakes with stolen molasses away from the fire, while Lainey entered enthusiastically into the discussion.

It was a cheerful evening, for there had been no sign of pursuit since they crossed the Namoi. The horses were quiet after two days of heavy going, sometimes churning across muddy channels and black soil plains, and they caused little stress as they spread out to feed, accompanied by the occasional tinkle of a hobble chain and night bell.

'I wish I'd learned more about thievin' when I was younger,' Lainey said to Will, with a note of censure in her voice. 'You never did let me join in, an' now I've got so much to learn — I wanna be useful for more than just tailing horses. Next time you rob somethin' you'd better let me in on it.'

'Thievin' ain't hard,' said Will. 'You just take it steady — hold yer nerve. Know when to move and when to stand still — it's amazing how hard it is to see a man,' he looked at Lainey, 'or woman, who freezes every muscle in the shadows. One time I was crossin' through a back yard tryin' to get away from a coupla fellas I'd been gamblin' with, when a cove came out for a piss. I stood still next to 'is clothesline, not a yard away while 'e did is business. He was so close that when 'e burped I could smell the poached eggs he'd et for tea, and still 'e didn't see me.'

'It's settled then,' said Lainey. 'Next time you rob somethin' I'm comin' too. 'Ow am I gonna learn if I don't?'

★ ★ ★ ★ ★

North of Collarenebri they ignored the main route along the Barwon and cut north through scrubby country on a lesser-known track that led to a series of lagoons and clay pans that Jim called Mungeroo Warrambool.

Now only fifty miles from the Queensland border it was starting to look like they might make it in a single day's ride. Walking the horses twenty yards then trotting twenty – Will estimated that they were making a good six miles an hour.

They stopped for dinner camp, hobbling the horses and letting them roam over a goose-picking of grass on a burned plain studded with trees, small but abrupt hills and scrub.

Soon after reaching the spot, Jim, who had been quiet for the last hour or two, slipped away on foot, and returned some twenty minutes later.

'Sam nearly ate your share a' lunch Jim,' said Will. 'That's what happens when you wander off like that.'

Jim didn't laugh but sat down with his back to a tree trunk and began to eat. He had never learned table manners, and ate with his mouth open, giving a good demonstration of the process of mastication.

'What's wrong with you?' Will asked. 'Got an ear-ache?'

'I seen eagle again, bloke – different one now, but he knows me. Someone's on our trail — clever barsted too. Not movin' up too fast. I just went back and climbed one a' them hills, and I seen a pall of smoke hangin' over some trees way back — like someone lighted just enough of a fire to boil a billy then put it out straight away.'

'Long Douglas?' suggested Sam.

Will blew threw his teeth. 'I can't believe that anyone would use the words Long Douglas an' clever in the same speech.'

Sam shrugged, 'Maybe your own people, Jim?'

'Nah, not them,' said Jim. 'I might ride back further and see if I can spot them, then catch up with youse again.'

'Fair enough,' said Will, 'but don't start any gunfights.'

Jim inclined his head, pulled his hat down and went to catch his horse. The others followed suit.

'If it's true that there might be someone behind us,' said Will. 'We'd best get some miles down too.'

★ ★ ★ ★ ★

The country altered little as they rode on that afternoon, and they missed Jim's quiet bushcraft as they closed in on the Queensland border. Will had expected his mate back by mid-afternoon, but it was after four when the Gamilaroi man rode back in, with a thoughtful expression on his face.

As if by agreement they reined in together, the sound of horses taking the opportunity to munch on the grass the only accompaniment to their voices.

'So, what's goin' on?' asked Will.

'There's two men on our trail, bloke. One white man, big-feller with a wide hat and one a' them fancy moustaches. The other is his tracker, maybe Wiradjuri-feller from south of home, but strange thing — wearing spectacles like a white man. You ever seen a tracker wearin' specs?'

'I 'ave,' said Lainey. 'But it can't be 'im. Police, d'ya think?'

Jim just shook his head. 'Not traps, but they follerin' our sign.'

Lainey started to say something, then stopped, so they all looked at her.

'What?' asked Will.

'Nothin''

'What if it's someone after that dead man's letter?' said Jim. 'The thing that you found in Clarkie's saddle bags.'

'Holy cow! That's a thought,' said Will.

'Best thing to stop and ambush 'em,' said Sam.

'True,' Will mused. 'If it's just two of them we'll 'ave no issue wrappin' them up.'

'We 'ave to stop them from follerin' us somehow,' said Jim, 'and if they ain't traps there's nothing to stop them goin' all the way up into Queensland after us.'

'How far behind are they?' asked Will.

Jim indicated an arc of the sun's movement with his hand, that Will translated as roughly an hour.

'Let's lay a trail 'til we see a good spot,' he said. 'Then we'll double back an' Lainey can wait up ahead with the 'orses.'

'What?' spat Lainey, 'you won't let me be part of this damned show?'

Will scowled, 'This is serious business, an' you still aren't fully over that fall. For that matter, can ya stop swearin' for Chrissakes? 'Ow many times do I 'ave to tell you?'

Lainey flicked her reins and rode on, plainly annoyed, and the others followed. They didn't have long to wait before the cattle pad they were following wound past a low hillock with a sharp escarpment at the northern end. There was also a large tree for cover.

As planned, they rode on for another quarter mile, at which point Lainey, still complaining, took the horses ahead while the men doubled back on foot.

Once in the chosen spot they took their positions with their rifles ready. Will sat down on the far side of the tree, wishing for a smoke but knowing he couldn't until this job was done.

He was in full view of Sam, who had moved another fifty paces up the track, and hidden himself. Jim, meanwhile, had scampered up the slope to keep watch.

'After they come, you wait until I give the word,' Will called.

Sam stuck his thumb behind his front teeth and flicked it forwards, an obscene gesture he had picked up from somewhere and Will hated.

'You can stop that attitude right now,' called Will. 'Someone's gotta call the shots around here. You an' Jim couldn't pluck a chook without me.'

Sam made a face but said nothing, settling down on his rump to wait, pulling a tiny Chinese book from a pocket and beginning to read. Will was less patient, picking up tiny stones and throwing them at a nearby bull-ant nest. This, unfortunately, had the effect of increasing the level of activity from the ants. Their erratic zigzag running doubled in speed, and they began to come uncomfortably close.

Will had just stood up to get away from the insects, when Jim came scrabbling back down the slope, calling out, 'Close now orright. They comin'.'

Will checked the round in the chamber of the Snider and waited. Before too long he heard the clip of a horse at a fast walk, and ahead of it a light-footed tread. This latter sound was made by the tracker — bespectacled just as Jim had reported.

The instant the tracker came into view his eyes locked on Will, and he turned on his heel to retreat.

'Stop there,' Will cried, emerging with the carbine held steady, the butt between bicep and trunk. He was now able to see not just the tracker but a well-dressed man on horseback.

When Jim wandered out, just as well-armed, both the travellers looked for a line of retreat down the track, but that was when Sam moved to block their way from behind.

Will levelled his carbine at the tracker. 'You lay on the ground. Now!' He continued to cover the man until he was stretched out, face-down on the earth.

Now Will walked up towards the horseman. 'Who

the hell are you and why are you follerin' us?'

It was obvious at first glance that the man was a gentleman, for he wore good trousers, a waistcoat and embossed-leather boots that extended to his calf. The second glance was more telling. When Will looked into those brown eyes he recognised the man with a confused jolt.

'Blarsted what?' he exclaimed. 'I know you. Luke Phillips ain't it?'

The man on horseback looked back levelly. He was an imposing-looking man, with a jaw like a dressed-stone block. 'And I know you, Will Jones. I've come for my wife and to fetch her back home. If you'll tell your mates to put their guns away, I'd like you to take me to Elaine as speedily as you can.'

Will lowered the muzzle of his rifle until it pointed at the ground. 'Well, I 'ave to respect you blokes,' he said, with a sweeping glance to take in the bespectacled Aboriginal man, 'who 'as tracked us so well.' He paused and rummaged in his pockets for a pipe and pouch. 'I can take you to Lainey, but I wouldn't hold out too much for your chances of gettin' her to leave. She's startin' to think she's Captain Thunderbolt.'

'Well, she's not,' said Luke Phillips. 'She's my wife and she needs to come home.'

★ ★ ★ ★ ★

Will gave the married couple an hour to sort out their differences, but this was never going to be sufficient. The hour turned into a full evening of stops and starts and shouts and brief interludes of hugging. At one stage Phillips threatened that if she made him ride off alone, he'd turn them all in to the first trap he saw.

Meanwhile, Will, Jim, Sam, and the tracker with his glasses, who went by the white name of Josiah, sat miserably, staring at the fire, while the drama played out on the fringes of the camp. Every word, unfortunately for the listeners, was audible.

'I aren't goin' back,' Lainey said repeatedly.

'Well, why not? Haven't I been good to you?'

'You 'ave been good. But that ain't enough. You don't let me *do* anyfink. I get bored jest sittin' around the whole time.'

'Listen, your brother's wanted for murder. You say he didn't do it, but if they catch you all and bang him up, they'll hang you for being an accessory.'

'I'd rather die with me boots on, with me comrades of the track, than waste away in a drawin' room drinkin' cups of tea in fine china and listenin' to Miss Arsewipe from Coona play the pianner.'

'Oh Elaine, can't you understand that I love you?'

'I understand that, well enough, but you still ain't givin' me an option worth thinkin' on. We're riding for

Queensland at dawn, and you ain't coming with us.'

'I'll follow, Elaine, you can't stop me. I'll follow you until the world ends.'

★ ★ ★ ★ ★

In the late evening a dry wind sprang up from the north-west, from the vastness of outback Queensland and beyond.

Elaine's heart had been seized by that restless wind, and it seemed that she believed in that moment that she could have the things she wanted and leave those that she would rather not have behind. In those hours she was a queen, and all men her belongings.

Sometime around midnight, Elaine came into camp and fetched her bedroll. Within a few minutes the sounds of lovemaking emanated from the outer camp. This soon subsided, and everyone managed to get some sleep.

Before dawn, Elaine was already dressed, waking the others with a whispered, 'Let's get out of here.'

Before they rode off Will went to see to the welfare of Lainey's husband, Luke Phillips. Knowing him for a sound sleeper, Elaine had tied him up in his sleep, trussed him like a pig ready for slaughter. Now, of course, he was awake and about as happy as a dingo with one foot in a spring-trap.

Will sat with Josiah for a moment before they left. 'Give us an hour or two before you untie him. We're riding hell for leather for the border and not stopping again. The traps won't be far behind now.'

Lainey had not gagged her man, and she bent to kiss him on the cheek before riding away. And as they worked the creaks out of the leather, heading north, he continued to scream out his love for her and intention that they be together again soon.

'One question, Lainey,' Will asked presently. 'If you wanted to be shot of old Luke, why'd you play the beast with two backs with 'im last night.'

Lainey shrugged as she rode, a wistful look on her face. 'Well, I felt sorry for the poor barsted, a' course. He'd ridden all this way. Besides,' she added with a wicked gleam in her eye, 'Luke sure does pack out his underwear.'

'Not another word,' Will said, then dropped back to ride with Sam.

9

THEY CROSSED the Queensland border late in the day and celebrated with a bottle of whisky that Lainey had taken from her husband's supplies.

''E likes the good stuff,' she said.

Will shrugged, 'Grog all tastes the same to me – burns me tongue and muddles me brain.' He took a long sip, coughed, and smiled. 'That's not to say I don't like the stuff, but rich man's grog don't impress me any more than ol' grandma's corn mash from a still hidden in the dairy.'

The one bottle, split between four of them, was enough to cheer the campfire that night, along with relief, particularly in Will's mind, to have escaped the colony of New South Wales and its undeserved price on his head. He fetched the stitched-canvas parcel from his saddlebag and turned it over and over in his hands. 'Now that we're in Queensland we'll be well-advised to keep our noses clean and hopefully the traps will stay off our backs.'

Lainey spat in disgust, presumably at this unexciting aspect to the plan, but Will carried on regardless. 'From 'ere we ride out west to this Kyungra Station, find this Joe McCartney and collect our one hundred pounds. Then we lay low, get some work until we've made a decent cheque, then I at least plan to amble north for a look.'

'Should we try an' disguise ourselves or somefink?' Lainey asked.

Fat Sam shook his head but pointed to Will's naval jacket. 'More better you stop wearin' that.'

'Good thinkin', Sam,' said Lainey, then to Will, 'It's on your bloody poster — last seen wearin' a naval officer's blue serge jacket. So, it would be best not to prance around in the darn thing.'

Will reluctantly agreed, folding the treasured garment deep in one of the main packs, finding himself a woollen overshirt to wear instead. He wasn't happy though, muttering bits and pieces about 'feeling naked without that blessed jacket.'

* * * * *

The following morning, they saddled up early, riding north to Dirranbandi. This was ground they had covered before, on the occasion that they had sold stolen horses in St George. When they reached the main road and turned west, they were in good spirits. They avoided police, Chinese, or any group that looked even faintly official, but this happened only rarely.

On the plains near Bollon, they joined up with a short-handed drover's crew on the stock route west. The boss was aptly named Smiley Robinson, for a grin never left his face, surrounded as it was by sandy-blonde hair and oversized listening tackle.

Smiley, it seemed, never said a bad word about anyone or anything. Not the laziest stockman or the one with the sharpest tongue. Even the worst behaved cows in the herd, (for it was breeders on the drive) kept his affection. 'Ah she's just a bit of a scallawag,' or another, well known for starting up a 'rush' he referred to as having a 'nervous disposition but that aren't her fault.'

For two weeks the little band fitted themselves into the drovers' schedule — starting before dawn, walking cattle all morning, dinner camp, more droving, then supper and taking turns on night watch. Lainey, in charge of tailing the horses, rose even before the rest of them.

It was slow going, no more than ten miles a day, but it was an opportunity to drop out of circulation. Besides, Will loved cattle work, and Jim was a natural. Sam more than earned his wage with his cooking, butchering and tailing. He was darn good on a horse into the bargain.

Reaching the Warrego, on the western side of Cunnamulla, Smiley Robinson paid them off, and said goodbye, for he and his crew were turning north towards Longreach. It was only now that Will asked for directions to Kyungra Station.

'What d'ye want to go there for?' asked Smiley Robinson.

'Just an errand.'

'Well, it's just about as far west as stations go, but if you really want to get there keep riding on from here. You've got Bow Creek, Sheep Station, the Paroo — now mind there can be fifty or more dry miles between each river and creek. You'll strike the Bulloo just south of Thargomindah, and you should follow it west until as far as Kulki Creek. Kyungra is just west of that junction, on a billabong they call the Dragon-lily. You ever been to the Channel Country?'

'Never.'

'Well, you're in for an eye-opener. Kyungra is west of the best part of it though, and on most of the run it's only bore-sinking that lets them operate. The place is owned by a fella called Joe McCartney.'

Will's ear pricked up at the name, for Joe McCartney was the man the package was addressed to. 'What's he like?'

Smiley just kept on smiling, and never said another

word. It was the first time Will had not heard him say something good about someone.

★ ★ ★ ★ ★

By the time they reached Eulo, supplies were again running low, and Will decided to risk going into town with Lainey, insisting that she wear a bonnet and look the part. In keeping with their desire not to commit any crime in Queensland, it seemed best to buy the things they needed.

Fat Sam and Jim were happy to stay in camp on the Paroo, for both were keen anglers, and they had already caught one fat yellowbelly using a grasshopper for bait.

Once Will and Lainey were mounted, and riding towards town, he said to her, 'If anyone asks, just say that you're my wife.'

'Yech,' she spat.

'Everyone knows that a murderer from Northern New South Wales is on the run with his sister. Just say it, will you?'

'If I 'ave to. But I think I'd've rathered stay in camp. Apart from anyfink it's so bloody stinkin' hot, and still as death.'

'If you want to be a bushranger, you'll 'ave to toughen yer hide, and learn to play a few parts. You get away with more from a few pretty lies than gun play.'

'I'll show you,' she said. 'I can lie better than just about anyone when I get warmed up.' She paused, 'An' if yer pretending to be me 'usband you can't go visiting any brothels.'

Will stiffened, 'I wouldn't think of doin' any such thing.'

Lainey made a face. 'Like 'ell you wouldn't. You've been handin' out yer hard-earned to five-shillin' scrubbers since you was fifteen.'

As they rode into town, Will noticed straight off that there was a crowd gathered in the main street, surrounded as it was by sun-faded timber facades — a true verandah post town.

First letting the horses drink at the public trough, then utilising the hitching posts nearby, Will and Lainey walked over to the crowd. In the centre a man wearing a muffin cap and dusty moleskins was talking, holding in his hands what appeared at first to be a lump of stone, but when the sun caught it a rainbow of colours shone forth in all directions.

Lainey hissed in her breath at the sight of it, and both she and Will tuned their ears to the man's words. His voice was strangely educated, belying the dishevelled nature of his clothing.

'They're calling it boulder opal,' said the man. 'And there's only one place in the world where it's been found — right here in south-western Queensland. The market

is still being developed, but mark my words: this is goin'
to make people rich, and right 'ere in Eulo …'

'Who made you the farkin' expert?' someone called
out.

'I'm a geologist,' said the man, 'trained at Sydney
University, and I've got no vested interest except that
the more people who get out and find this stuff the
better chance we have of developing markets. I've hired
a private room at the Eulo Hotel yonder and for anyone
who wants to learn more I'll be there at seven tonight.'

'Are ya buyin' us supper mate?' another wag called
out.

'No, but every man,' his eyes rested on Lainey, 'or
woman who wishes to learn more about this boulder
opal racket and comes along will get a small piece of
opal for themselves, to take away at no charge.'

After the delivery of this piece of information the
geologist shrugged off further questions, and with the
shouted repetition of 'Seven o'clock tonight,' he carried
his boulder opal away towards the hotel. A few of the
crowd carried on after him.

'I wouldn't mind a bit of that opal rock,' said Lainey,
''ave you ever seen anyfink so beautiful?'

'I'd like to learn more about minin' the stuff,' said
Will. 'I might just ride back at seven tonight and listen
to the man talk. You can 'ave me share of the rock he
said he'd give out.'

'You're very kind sir,' said Lainey, bunging on a lady's voice. Then, 'Just make sure that you pick me out a good one.'

★ ★ ★ ★ ★

Inside the store they bought no luxuries, just flour, salt, tea, tobacco and Lea and Perrins sauce, while Lainey flirted with the assistant in an effort to squeeze a few bob out of the price.

On the way out, heavily laden with the supplies as they were, a man in a high cap, woollen trousers and jacket showing the insignia of the Queensland Mounted Police was standing in the middle of the street. He had a neat and compact figure, and an unusually white face amongst the generally sun-browned or indigenous locals.

The Queensland trap tipped his hat at Lainey then addressed Will. 'Afternoon, good fellow,' he said.

'Afternoon,' said Will, and went to move on past.

'You're not from around these parts,' said the policeman.

'No,' said Will. 'Me wife and I are from out east — come here to look around, maybe dig for some of them boulder opals.'

'Ye staying in the hotel?' asked the trap.

'No, camped out of town.'

'Well, my name's Constable Wright. What's yours?'

Will had never been short of a *nom de guerre*, and the first one that came to his mind dropped easily from his lips. 'I'm Joshua Fairdale, and this is me bride Ursula.'

'Ursula!' repeated Constable Wright. 'Is that a French name.'

'Not quite,' said Lainey, looking very pleased, 'but you're close. It's a Russian name. Me mother was Russian.'

'Interesting. The Crimea perhaps?'

'Oh no,' said Lainey. 'She was as honest as a lamb.'

Wright showed his teeth, and Will took this for a smile. He seemed friendly enough.

'I hope you enjoy your stay in our little town of Eulo,' said the trap, then tipped his hat and walked away.

Will exchanged a look with Lainey, then hurried towards the horses. The worried feeling this encounter gave him soon subsided, however, and by the time they reached the Paroo camp, with the smell of roasting fish in their nostrils, he was again thinking about riding back into town to learn more about opals.

'You see any Cantonese?' Sam asked.

'No, a couple with pig-tails was all. But a trap was a little interested in us. It's a shame, for I wouldn't mind going back in to hear a talk some cove is givin' about boulder opals and how a fella can make a bundle diggin' them up.'

'Yes, a darn shame,' said Lainey, 'and I would like a pretty rock like that for free – everyone who goes to the talk gets one.'

After a good meal of fish and damper, Fat Sam gave his opinion, 'More better we should pack up now and move on.'

'I dunno,' replied Will, 'I'm thinking that I might still ride in for the talk. It'll fit with me cover — looking around for opportunities. Hiding in camp is more like a man on the run would do.'

WILL DRESSED in his best clobber, still hardly George Street standard, but good enough for the occasion. He took one of the night horses rather than his best gelding, and a spare saddle, for it would have to be left in the hands of a stable for a couple of hours and he had no idea if the people involved could be trusted. Thus, lightly encumbered, he rode off to town. He paid threepence for a half-pail of oats and a supervised hitch for his horse, along with storage for his tack, then headed towards the hotel.

It was then that he felt the first real puff of a fragrant but very hot breeze blowing down through Leo Street. He worried that it might unsettle the plant a little but carried on. Being some quarter-hour early for the meeting he headed in for a throat-moistener.

The front bar of the Eulo Hotel was about what Will would have expected from an outback town. It was filled with characters of all types: brumby runners, dinger-baiters, ring-barkers, ringers and drovers; rubbing shoulders with bank-johnnies, stock agents, chalkies, chippies and businesspeople from the town.

Not everybody stopped nattering when Will walked in, but all eyes were on him. He ordered a pot of ale, a little warm for his taste but still the best thing that had passed his lips in many days. Thus engrossed, he stood at the bar and made occasional small talk with the tapman as he came and went to fill glasses with various brews.

He was halfway through his first when a frock-coated gentleman fronted the room and cleared his throat, announcing that anyone wishing to listen to the opal expert should come through, and that they were welcome to bring their drinks.

Will walked down the corridor, turned left through an open door, into a room lit by a chandelier holding some twenty or more candles, throwing dazzling light on a lectern and five rows of leather and timber seats. The attendees who were already there filled most of the front two rows. They were a mixed bunch — a few travelling jobbers, a couple of dusty stockmen, some young gentlemen and older local businessmen who obviously wanted to learn about this new industry and what angle they could take on it.

Will took a seat in the back row. It was a while since he had sat on anything but a stump, a saddle, the bare ground, a rock, or a bar stool, and he almost exclaimed aloud at the sheer comfort of the padded leather. Still holding his drink, he watched the opal man come in and arrange a few papers on the lectern, just as the final few attendees rolled in.

Last of all was none other than Constable Wright, who came through the door carrying a tumbler of whisky in one hand, doffing his cap as he entered, uncovering a close-shaven scalp with a dark birthmark above his right ear. His garibaldi jacket was newly laundered. This, decided Will, must be his dress uniform and looked very impressive indeed.

The policeman greeted every soul in the room in turn, for they all seemed to know him. He obviously had an interest in horse racing for he exchanged a few fragments on this topic with a well-built gentleman near the front, something about the rising odds of a favourite for an upcoming race meeting.

Finally, however, Wright walked through and took the vacant seat beside Will. The policeman smelled of Macassar oil and whisky, but his eyes were as clear as daylight.

'Evening Mister Fairdale, I'm glad to see you again. I do recall you saying that you are interested in the mining of boulder opal.'

Will was discomforted by the policeman's presence, but he was careful not to show it. 'I'd be a fool not to follow up on an opportunity. I've heard that men are gettin' rich down around Lightnin' Ridge. What about you? Thinkin' of givin' up on copperin' and makin' a few bob with a shovel?'

'Not really,' said Wright. 'But I like to keep my eye on the pulse of things. Where did you say you were from again?'

'I didn't say, I don't reckon, but me wife, ah Ursula and me are from Toowoomba.'

'Are you travelling alone — just the two of you, or are you in company?'

'Almighty Christ, that's a lot of questions. It's making me head spin.' Will turned his eyes to the front. 'Here, looks like old mate's about to start his talk.'

The talk began with a long-winded and technical explanation of how an opal gets formed, the speaker using his voice theatrically, something like a stage-magician, and his hands as theatre to explain.

'Water impregnated with silica flows and seeps into spaces in the ironstone, and there, over thousands, nay, millions of years ...'

At this stage he had to pause while someone in the audience asked him how this could be possible when, according to the Bible, the earth was only 6000 years old. This commenced a side-tracked discussion that ended with a theological argument, and finally the geologist brought that part of the talk to a close, handing out the fragments of boulder opal he had promised.

Each piece was around the size of a river pebble, but more jagged, and a thousand times prettier, catching the light of the candles. Will was deeply examining his, sure that Lainey was going to be appreciative of it, when Wright spoke again, in a very low voice, scarcely noticeable amongst the other punters making delighted noises at the fire in their stones.

'A strange thing, you know Mister Fairdale. I had a letter come through from Brisbane today, warning of a wanted man and his accomplices on the run from New South Wales.'

Will's breath caught in his throat. 'There's all types, aren't there? Vagabonds everywhere, an' lucky we have a police force of good men like you to hold 'em back.'

Wright appeared to ignore the comment. 'The interesting thing is that the wanted man – wanted for murder I might add – looks a lot like you.'

'Well,' said Will, starting to rise. 'I think I've learned enough about opals for one night. I'd best be going.'

'I wouldn't go too far tonight,' said Wright. 'The dust is blowing already. Looks like a bad one.'

Will, half out of his seat, hesitated, he had heard the wind rattling the window frames, but hadn't thought much of it. Even so, he began to make his way to the door.

Wright stood up also. 'I'll walk you to your horse.'

The geologist, who was just about to start the second portion of his lecture, looked put-out to be losing two of his patrons straight after handing out the inducements, but Will merely inclined his head in farewell, heading for the door with Wright very close on his heels as he walked down the corridor.

When Will reached the front door of the pub he found it closed tight, for outside the wind was blowing fiercely, and when he went to grip the handle two men in regular clothes disentangled themselves from the front bar and joined them near the door. Both held Webley 'second pattern' revolvers steady, aimed at Will's mid-section.

Wright turned to them, 'Thanks for your help gentlemen.' Then, to Will, 'It's a little hard sometimes, being the only officer of the law in this town. Luckily, I have some civic-minded friends who help me out. They're both fine pistol shots as well. I really think, Mister Fairdale, that you should come down to the station while we settle some doubt about your identity.'

11

The Eulo police station was constructed of timber slabs, rough-edged, the spaces plugged with clay mixed with cow-dung, though the wind could be heard howling outside. Clever shelving and wall-hooks gave the place a tidy air. The floor was of earth and ant-hill dirt, beaten together into a concrete-like hardness, and the air was oppressively hot, even now, well into the evening.

Will, still not cuffed or under arrest, sat at a table opposite Wright, who remained as polite as if he were a brother-in-law or neighbour. He had produced a poster with the New South Welshman's image on it, and his two civilian helpers agreed that the likeness was striking.

'You can see the position I'm in, can't you?' asked Wright. 'This man Will Jones is travelling with his sister, along with a Celestial and an Aborigine called Jim. Now you say that the woman I met today is your wife, but might it be that in fact you sprung from the same dam?'

'Well I wouldn't 'ave married her if that were the case, would I?' quipped Will.

Wright gave a wry smile. 'You're a humorous man, but I'm sorry to say that this isn't a joke. I'm alleging that the woman supposedly called Ursula is your sister as *opposed* to being your wife, not in addition to.'

'Surely you must've seen her wedding ring?' tried Will.

'I did, of course, but that doesn't mean that she's married to you.'

'Well, I say it's true, an' you 'ave no reason not to believe me.'

'You say that you're from Toowoomba. What's the name of the main street?'

'Why it's Cumberland Street, of course,' said Will, saying the first thing that came into his head.

Wright shook his head slowly, the beginnings of a triumphant smile on his lips. 'It's not. The main street of Toowoomba is Ruthven Street.'

'Well, some folks do say that,' said Will, 'but Cumberland runs into it — down near the post office.' He was banking on the unlikelihood of anyone there owning a map of the place.

The policeman and his mates shook their heads at each other, unable to disprove this conclusively and Wright carried on. 'Were you and ah, Ursula married in

Toowoomba?'

'No sir, we was hitched up in Brisbane.'

'What church?'

For this question Will was prepared. He had attended the funeral of his old man in that city, and he could picture the place of worship where it had been held in his mind as clear as day.

'All Saints in Spring Hill. Beautiful church it was too, and Ursula looked truly virginal, she did.' He lowered his voice, 'though we was never quite certain on that point I must say.'

'Where did you work in Toowoomba?'

'Labourer, at the brick factory. Well kind of a foreman really – one of them blokes what tells the other coves what to do.' He puffed out his chest and bunged on a voice, 'Work faster you lazy slugs. Make them bricks quicker.'

'I'm not aware of a brick factory in Toowoomba,' Wright observed.

Will's eyes widened, 'Oh yes, a'course there is. Just down the end of … Cumberland Street.'

Wright raised his eyebrows, 'Near the post office?'

'Nah, kind of down the other end. Near the bridge over the ah … river there.'

'The Condamine perhaps?' suggested Wright.

'Yes, a' course. That's it, the Condamine.'

'Mister Fairdale, I'm sorry to say that the Condamine

doesn't quite flow through Toowoomba. Gowrie Creek does.'

'That must have been it then.' Will slapped himself lightly on the scone with the tips of his fingers. 'Damn me for being a forgetful barsted.'

Wright stood up, and with his two deputies retreated to the far end of the room, where they talked in low voices. Will listened with interest, cursing the two small lumps of boulder opal that sat on the table — his and Wright's. It was that damned opal that had compelled him to ride back into town. It had been a stupid idea and he should have known better.

This thought led him to wonder what Lainey and the others would be thinking now that he had not come back. Fat Sam and Jim were both smart and cunning in their own ways, but Will was the one who made decisions — they'd be helpless without him, he knew that for a fact.

Wright let his deputies out by the front door, thanking them for their help, then addressed Will. 'I've no choice but to keep you in custody overnight. In the morning, provided the dust has dropped, I'll ride out with you and question your travelling companions. If everything checks out, you'll be set free.' Wright did not trouble to say what would happen if things didn't check out.

'That's bloody monstrous,' cried Will. 'I've done no

crime.'

'That may be so,' said Wright. 'But you'll spend tonight in the cell. I'll be in the bedroom just there, so I'll hear if you so much as scratch yourself.'

★ ★ ★ ★ ★

Will had experienced the sound of a slamming cell door before. It was not a pleasant sound, and repetition had not made it any more pleasing. It was a sound that he associated with bad food, casual bashings, certain disrespect, and most miserably, a lack of personal freedom.

There was only one cell, and it was tacked on to the back of the station like an outhouse. If the heat in the station itself had been extreme, here, Will decided, it was murderous. The cell was scarcely four paces by three, with a cot and mattress, a latrine bucket, and an unplumbed sink with a bucket of water. The door and walls were sheathed with iron sheet, apart from a judas' gate in the door and a window of interlocking steel mesh. This allowed the dust-laden wind from outside to enter in fits and starts, strong enough to have extinguished the candle that was burning inside when he first entered.

It was a lonely and unsettling place, but after a thorough investigation he saw little point in any attempt to break out. The cell was impregnable. He settled down onto the cot, and rested his head on the pillow, desperately unhappy and berating himself for being as big a fool as any that ever breathed.

To distract himself he tried to think about the girl he loved. Helen. The girl in the daguerreotype. Her perfect long hair and serene gaze. He imagined her voice, and the clever things she said. Imagined a farm homestead they might one day share together, welcoming guests and deciding whether to serve the roast mutton on the silver or porcelain.

He was tired, however, and his eyes had closed when he felt an itchy movement around his ankles and lifted that limb to scratch. Another movement. This time on his neck. Bedbugs. One of the many things he hated about sleeping inside. Leaving the pillow, he laid down on the hard floor beside the bed.

At length, still itching, he fell asleep, while the wind continued its howling outside.

★ ★ ★ ★ ★

A couple of hours later, Will never knew exactly how long, he was dreaming of a voice, but it was part-wind, part human, and he was reluctant to engage with it. Over and over, it called his name, until finally his eyes snapped open, and he rolled to his feet, aching in a hundred bones and muscles from the hard ground.

'Will,' came the hiss of a voice, 'answer me you darned idiot.'

Finally rousing himself, he identified the sound as having come from the window, and he moved across and put his face up close to the mesh. On the other side he could make out a female face that must be Lainey.

'Yeah, it's me,' he said.

'Thank Christ for that. We figured you must have been lagged. Took a lot of creepin' round in this damn dust to find this place though — lucky this ain't much of a town.'

'Thanks for lookin',' he said. 'It's like an oven in here.'

'Not much better out here,' she said. 'But listen. There's a blacksmith's shop and a shed next to it; looks vacant, just a little down the street. Jim's goin' to set it afire, directly, and start yellin' fit to wake the dead. Is there only one trap here, or two?'

Will sensed that Lainey was having the time of her life, playing the girl bushranger at last. 'One trap.'

'Good. As soon as 'e runs out the front door, we'll bust you out, right?'

'How?'

'No time now — I've got to get back to the plant. I'll be waiting just out of town. Go with Sam, he knows where.'

With those words she was gone, and Will sagged back to sit on the edge of the cot, waiting, adrenaline already shooting into his system. Every few minutes he stood and scanned out into the night, and he listened for any sound. All he heard, however, was the howling wind.

Will spent the next little while trying to define Lainey's use of the word 'directly.' That word could mean so much in different contexts, anything from 'as soon as I finish my smoke,' to 'next week.' Thinking of smoke made him wish for a calming pipe. He wasn't used to going long without tobacco and he didn't like the sensation.

Sweat was gathering in his armpits, running down his neck, between the muscles of his chest and in a line down his belly. More bedbugs joined him from the cot. The bloody things! He wondered how he and Helen would eradicate them from their bed when they were married. He hated the thought that the damn insects might scar the perfection of their life together.

He felt them stick in his sweat and become trapped. The imagined anguish of the sweat-bogged parasites gave his mind something to play on while he waited, and after a while, just for a moment, he forgot what was happening altogether.

It was only then that he began to smell smoke on the breeze – just a whiff from a wayward gust, and then a moment later a distant voice he knew well at full cry.

'Fire, hey. Help, fire!'

It was followed by the sound of running feet from inside the station, and then jangling keys and the front door flying open. This sound retreated, replaced by a new set of feet, then a sudden, surprising, resounding smash as something blasted into the door of his cell. On the second blow the head of a blacksmith's sledgehammer protruded through the metal skin, and on the third the door came off its hinges and sagged. The fourth blow was needed merely to clear the way.

Sam said nothing. Instructions were not necessary, as the Cantonese turned and took to flight towards the open front door with Will close on his heels. The air was all dust, smoke and confusion, and as they ran through the open front door, they had visibility enough to see the shed diagonally across the road thoroughly afire, with gangs of people on the roadway, someone organising a bucket chain, and the silhouette of a man who looked like it might be Wright facing the flames, not having yet turned to see them.

Will was a faster runner than Sam on his stubby legs, but he let the other man lead the way, not on the street itself, but the verge, where shrubs and other plants might help to screen them. They were out of sight of the fire when Will came to a sudden halt.

'Wait here,' he cried, 'I forgot somefink.'

'Idiot,' cried Sam. 'What you doing?'

But the words were lost on Will as he sprinted back through the murk, the way they had come. Seeing that Wright was still involved with the fire he tore back through the open front door of the station and reached the table where he had been questioned a few hours earlier. The two pieces of boulder opal were still sitting where they had been left. Will snatched both of them up, then tore out the door again, just as Wright turned away from the fire and looked towards him.

'Stop,' cried the policeman, but Will was only just getting into a gallop, tearing down the street with his arms pumping and his legs moving like the connecting-rods on a locomotive. He risked a look back and saw that Wright had hurried back into the station house, presumably to fetch a weapon. A hundred forceful yards further on and Will again reached Fat Sam's position.

'Fool,' hissed Sam again, as they ran neck and neck for the edge of town, and Jim came tearing down a side street to meet them, his bare chest shiny with sweat. The true athlete of the group, Jim could run like the wind when unencumbered.

On the fringes of town, before the river, Jim led them down a side-track, it being almost impossible to navigate in the dark and heavy dust away from the lantern-lit town. Only the Gamilaroi man's highly tuned skills allowed them to find their way.

Up ahead were the dull shapes of horses, and Lainey herself, with night horses tacked up, and Will's saddle ready. The spare he had ridden to town on was still at the stables and trying to retrieve it was out of the question.

Within a minute, they were ambling away to the west, with Jim in the front, his unerring sense of direction their only hope. The dust was a terror and a curse: awful to ride in, and the horses hated it, but they would leave no tracks; no trace as they rode, and surely no one would try to follow until it had settled.

It was only after they had covered an uncomfortable half-mile that Will called out his thanks to the others for his rescue. 'Well done, you lot. It weren't any picnic in that cell.'

'It was Fat Sam, who guessed what had happened an' had the plan,' Lainey said.

'It were a good plan, thanks,' said Will. 'I know I should 'ave listened when you said that goin' to town was not a good idea.' Then, to Lainey. 'I told some good fibs back there at the station – how you an' me was married in Brisbane, and all about Toowoomba – a town where I've never been. I wish you could've heard me – I was dressin' untruths up in vestments fit fer a prince and sprinklin' them with gold dust.'

'Well, it must've worked a treat,' said Lainey, 'seein'

as how they locked you up in a cell.'

Jim laughed at this, but the irony seemed to be lost on Will, for he carried on talking as if she had paid him a compliment. 'Shame we left a good night horse behind in them stables – and a saddle, but it could've been much worse.' At that moment he remembered the two lumps of boulder opal in his pocket. Removing both items, he rode close to Lainey so she could take them off his hands. 'These are for you,' he said, 'all them birthdays I've missed, all in one hit.'

'Hope you like 'em,' called Fat Sam. 'Silly bugger Will went back for 'em. Trap not even seen us 'til then.'

Lainey smiled through the dark and dusty night at her brother. 'Well, that's nice. Gratefully accepted an' I'll 'ave a good look at them when we get out of this blessed dust.'

12

THAT RIDE to the west was no picnic. The dust stopped blowing by mid-afternoon the next day, but they hadn't sighted surface water since Eulo, and the horses were on the way to perishing when they found a bore-fed government trough not long after dark.

With a good supply of tucker, tea and tobacco, they agreed to avoid all towns from that time on. That was easy enough for there wasn't a village worthy of the name for a hundred miles.

'That fella s' posed to give us one hunnerd-pound for this trip getting' it cheap,' opined Fat Sam. 'Worth two hunnerd, I reckon.'

Gamilaroi Jim was more cheerful. Once the dust storm had settled, leaving big, clear skies, he liked this kind of country, and enjoyed encountering new bird calls to learn and mimic – green budgerigars in their creek-side flocks, two or three new varieties of parrots and spinifex pigeons.

The country never stayed the same but changed constantly — sometimes thick with mulga trees and at others plains of blue, mitchell or flinders grasses. Sometimes they crossed gibber country with stones that rolled and rubbed beneath the horses' hooves. They encountered the first extensive inland lake system of the journey – Lake Bindegolly – fringed by orange sand, and its waters lying deathly still: watercolour sunsets reflected as if by a mirror.

Long days of riding followed, with the usual problems of lame mounts, saddle galls and lack of water at the right times of day. They gave station homesteads and stock camps a wide berth, but they did ride in on a bore-sinking crew who had struck hot artesian water at depth, and after washing all the horses, then soaking saddle cloths and beating them dry, they all availed themselves of a bogey, with Lainey insisting that Will guard her privacy with his rifle.

The bore crew were working with the assistance of a Robey portable steam engine, fuelled with dry mulga logs, and Will thought it was grand how it drove sections of pipe underground and tapped into ancient water supplies far below the earth.

He had little fear of the crew giving them away, for the boss told them straight off that, 'We ain't seen a soul for six weeks.'

They stayed three nights, and before they rode off Will left their new mates with a good supply of tobacco. 'If a trap happens to ride along this way, would you tell 'em you 'aven't seen us?' Will knew for a fact that Constable Wright would be riding after them. Traps never let anything slide, especially when they have been made fools of.

'I won't tell them nothin', said the team boss. 'Not fond of the barsteds meself.'

★ ★ ★ ★ ★

Like all journeys, including that of life itself, the days went on with their small crises, minor adventures, and scrapes. Jim shot a branded 'killer' on a big run, and they were still burning the bones and hides, curing strips, and filling their stomachs with fresh meat when a station hand rode in.

'Hey, whose beast is that you're eating?'

'Just a kangaroo,' said Will standing to meet him.

The stockman caught sight of the size of the bones still smouldering on the fire. 'Damn big kangaroo,' he scoffed.

'Monster,' said Will. 'Never seen another one like it.'

On another day Lainey was bailed up by a couple of dingos when she was at her morning ablutions and ran yelling back into camp – still not quite properly attired.

This incident gave them all a laugh.

'Next time,' she said to Will, 'you can stand guard.'

Will made a face. 'Why do I have to guard you all the time? I'm not yer damned husband. You 'ad one an' you didn't want 'im so I don't see why I should play hero for ya.'

'At least I caught meself a man in the first place – which is more than I can say about your luck with women.'

Will snapped his fingers, 'I could get a fine wife just like that if I wanted.'

Lainey made a sly smile. 'Well, why don't you, instead of moonin' about that girl in the damned pitcher you carry everywhere?'

'One day I'll meet Helen face to face,' said Will, 'an' I'll marry her. You'll see.'

Fat Sam had been watching, his arms folded. 'More better you eat breakfast so we can strike camp,' he said.

★ ★ ★ ★ ★

Slowly they made their way west, skirting south of Thargomindah where they met the Bulloo River. There Will saw the first camel train of his life, with a taciturn Afghan walking alongside, and the huge creatures craning their elongated necks in curiosity as they passed.

On a wide Bulloo waterhole Sam and Jim found success with their fishing lines, pulling in a couple of good perch for the pan. The going was easier, following that ancient riverbed from hole to hole, with the dried clay easy going in between.

All the while corellas nested in boles and hollows, squawking in their thousands, with a far greater claim of being owners of this country than the very few whites around the place. Wedge-tailed eagles, more numerous than their cousins in the faraway Warrumbungles, were almost always overhead, hunting and studying the vast domain below, and Jim raised his eyes to watch them now and then.

Keeping Smiley Robinson's instructions in mind, Will kept an eye out for the junction with Kulki Creek. Knowing that it was a substantial waterway, he identified it accurately when the time came, for they reached it late in the day. They camped amongst the river red gums and coolabah trees and turned west the following day.

The realisation that they were on Kyungra Station came when they reached a stock camp hard at work with a bronco panel, branding stock.

A bronco panel was a set of sloped poles with a notch, over which a rope stretched, attached to a young cow or bull at one end, and a horse at the other. The rope could be dragged by the rider until it fitted into the notch, holding the beast immobile while the team roped the legs and prepared it for branding or gelding.

Will and the others dismounted to watch, not wanting to interrupt. They had been seen, of course, but the ringers involved would wait for a break in proceedings before coming across to talk.

Finally, when a young bull was carefully released, newly parted with his gonads and the brand still smoking on his rump, the team boss walked over to greet them. He looked gaunt but capable, wearing concertina leggings, a loose shirt and a neckerchief.

Will stepped up to meet him and shook a hand as hard as iron. 'G'day, my name's Will Jones,' he said. Lying to traps was one thing. Lying to working men another. 'Is this Kyungra Station?'

'Sure is. I'm Fred Chancey, head stockman.'

'And Joe McCartney is the owner?'

'That's correct too.'

'He's the one we need to see, would ya mind drawin' us a mud-map to the homestead?'

Chancey crinkled up his eyes. 'Well, I could, but tell me, are you and your mates clued up for stock work?'

Will shrugged, 'We've all done a bit.'

'Then I'll go one better than a mud map – I'll take you to the homestead myself. But listen, we're skint at least two men here. I'd count it as a big favour if you give us a hand for the arvo then we'll ride in together later.'

It was obvious that the crew were short-handed, with a mob of clean skins yarded in a rough enclosure of bush poles. They were mostly yearlings or better, growing angry in the heat. The men were lean, harried, but serious workers, experts at the task.

'My oath we'll help,' cried Will. 'Give us a minute to dump our blasted gear and we'll get on top of these buggers in no time.' And not wasting any time, they set up camp under a tree, hobbled the horses they didn't need and set off with stock saddles and ropes.

Will and Jim, at least, had plenty of experience with a bronco panel, and were more than happy to put their skills to use. The panel had been constructed in a natural clearing, and the dust of raised hoofs rose into the sky. The smell of bovine dung and sweating hides hit the senses.

'Righto, you blokes,' Will said, including Lainey in this statement. 'We know this caper backwards. Sam, stand off to get the bolters, Jim you give the roper a spell, and Lainey and I'll help with the branding iron.

In the time it takes to smoke a pipe the operation was moving twice as fast as it had before the arrival of Will and his mates. The cattle were of mixed hereford, angus and shorthorn ancestry, some brindled, some mottled, others dull grey, and others brown and white. All wore a layer of dust and had fed-up eyes. Few wanted to play the game nicely.

Even the smallest weaner had attitude, and while Jim was as good a roper as any man down Pilliga way even Will was soon in awe at the skills of the man his mate was matched with.

Within moments they were earning their salt – Lainey gathered fresh and dry wattle timber and fanned the fire, then whetted her knife and gelded young bulls as they went down.

Sam was soon in pursuit of a recalcitrant heifer, his horse making long-legged strides across that dusty proving-ground, for all the men were watching, some who had never seen a Cantonese man doing stock work before. Amusement turned to interest, then respect, as Sam roped her neatly, dragging her back across to the yards.

All afternoon it went on – blood, dust, heat and sweat. Yet, it was near sundown when the last of the yarded mob were branded, and they rode back in company with the station men. Will noticed more than a few interested glances thrown Lainey's way.

'I'll give you fair warnin', she's married,' said Will.

'Married, well,' one of them said. 'Where's yer husband then?'

'Oh, she left him behind,' Will explained. 'Too quiet for her, she reckons.'

Lainey slapped her brother on the rump with the butt of her stockwhip. 'I'll give you too quiet,' she said.

'Better than a big fat mouth that don't know when to shut up.'

The stockmen laughed, but then, as they skirted a very low, drying out waterhole, the sight of a homestead and station outbuildings appeared up ahead.

'Let's sort these horses out,' said the head stockman, 'and I'll introduce you to the boss. I think he owes you all a feed after what you did this arvo. But to be honest, he ain't the most friendly dog in the yard, not by a long shot.'

Will reflected on these words as they watered the horses at a long trough, fed by a creaking windmill from the billabong. Next, they removed saddles and bridles, and brushed their horses down before letting them run with the others to a round yard where fresh fodder had been strewn around.

'They've earned a feed,' said Chancey.

Leaving the others with the plant, Will took the package from his saddlebags, and started walking with the head stockman across the dusty track that surrounded the station buildings.

The homestead was a slab-sided place, as neat as a bush house could be, with a roof of thatched grass and a long verandah. A gardener stood up to watch as they passed, touching his hat.

'Afternoon, Simon,' called Chancey. 'Good work there mate.'

By the time they reached the house, a very tall lean man in his late forties had come out to watch them. He ignored Will at first and addressed his head stockman.

'Afternoon Fred, who's the strangers?'

'Mister McCartney, this here bloke says that he's come here to see you – an' ridden a long way by the sounds of it.'

McCartney squirted a mouthful of chewing tobacco into the azaleas in front of the verandah. 'What the hell are ya doin' bringin' vagrants in?' he asked. 'From what I see there's a Chinaman, a black, and this useless-lookin' piece of shit. Not to mention a white woman to cause fights and trouble like they allus do.'

'They're good people, sir – been helpin' all arvo with the brandin,' Chancey said.

'There's no spare money for extra wages,' said McCartney, then addressed Will. 'An' you can get your damn horses out of my yards – that lucerne cost me thirty pounds a ton landed, and I won't 'ave stranger's nags chewin' on it.' He paused. 'You say you came here to see me. State your business then piss orf.'

Will lifted the canvas-wrapped parcel with his right hand. 'This package is addressed to you. I'll read it. "To whomsoever will deliver this unopened to Joe McCartney at Kyungra Station will be given a reward of one hundred pounds. It is full restitution of all debts owed. LHD."'

McCartney's face went through a strange transition. At first a level of shock, his eyes hard as pebbles, then growing amusement. At length he burst out laughing. 'Sounds like a trick to me. Give it here. I'll open it first, and then I'll tell you if it's worth sixpence, let alone a hunnerd pounds.'

Will shook his head. 'No mate. I ain't stupid. You give me the money, and I'll give you the package.'

McCartney raised a frown that made his forehead look like the treeless ranges around Gundagai. 'I'm warnin' you, fella. That package has my name on it. That makes it my damn property.'

'Hundred pounds first,' said Will, 'or I'm keeping it.'

'You expect me to hand over a hunnerd pounds for somethin' I ain't expectin' and don't care about? For all I know it could be a trick you an' yer mates dreamed up.'

Will narrowed his eyes. 'I reckon you know who this LHD is. I seen you look funny when I said it.'

'Maybe I do and maybe I don't. Just give me the damn package, and I'll tell you if I think it's worth anything.'

'No,' said Will with a pugnacious tilt to his chin. 'I've ridden eight hundred miles, and I won't hand it over for nothing.'

McCartney lifted his chin. 'Take your letter, your woman, your Chinaman, and your boy, and get the hell off my land. An' if your horses aren't out of my yard in five minutes flat, I'll shoot them meself.'

Will opened his mouth to speak again, but he caught a warning glance from the head stockman, then a quick tap on the arm. Joe McCartney had already moved back through the door and into the house.

★ ★ ★ ★ ★

'I'm sorry about that,' said Fred Chancey as they walked back to the yards. 'But you really got the boss rattled with that package of yours. Any idea what's in it?'

'None at all, but me an' the others will need to have a talk about what to do next. If he won't pay, then we might just open it up and split it between us. We'll see.'

'I wish I had a couple more days with your crew on the job with us,' Chancey said. 'We'd nearly get through the rest of the branding, but the boss didn't seem likely to put you blokes on, even though we're short-handed.'

'Why so short-handed?'

'Not many men can cope with the boss, as you might understand – he can be a mean bastard. The quarters are rough and the tucker's worse. There's a lot of history – things in his past that seems to make 'im bitter. He hasn't been off this station since he bought it, ten or twelve year ago as far as I know.'

'See what 'appens,' said Will, 'but we'll help you out

if we can.'

★ ★ ★ ★ ★

When Will reached the yards, where the others were waiting, he could see from their glum expressions that they had already noticed that he was still carrying the package and wasn't in possession of a hundred pounds in cash.

'My advice,' said Chancey, 'is to head down along the creek bed a few hundred yards – there's another, smaller hole there. Hobble the horses out on the far bank, there's enough stubble to keep them alive, that's all, but at least they'll have water. Being out of sight the boss might forget about you, while you rest up.'

'Thanks,' said Will, and he shook the head stockman's hand, before heading back over to the yards to grab the horses and fill the others in on Joe McCartney's refusal to part with the promised fee.

'So, what are we gonna do?' asked Lainey.

'We'll go into camp and have a yarn about it,' said Will. 'If he doesn't want the damned package, we might finally just open it up ourselves. Though it seems a shame to do that after riding all this way.'

13

THE NEW CAMP was a good one, situated on the high bank on the far side, alongside a string of puddles a man could chuck a stone over without trying. The edges were dried hard and pock-marked from hooves.

With the horses hobbled out and a cooking fire of coolabah branches settling into coals, the company sat down together while Sam made damper and brewed a billy of tea. By the time the sun went down Will had just about determined that he would open the package then and there and split the contents.

'The old bugger won't pay,' said Will, 'so we might as well get somefink for our troubles – 'ere I am with a murder rap and escapin' lawful custody in Queensland to boot.'

Fat Sam had been sitting back, smoking a thoughtful pipe, the smoke curling out from his nose in twin streams. 'Back in China when I was a boy my pa used to tell a yarn about a young man who fell in love with daughter of richest man in the village. He were poor but wise, an' when he asked rich man if he could marry girl rich man say, *Never. No way.*

'Well, poor young fella was a wise bugger, an' he say, *I smart and one day I be rich. I love your daughter truly an' she love me. She will be happy. Will you reconsider?*

'*No, I will not, says rich man.*

'Poor young man say, *That your first chance. You will only get three.*

'Exactly one week later, poor man come back. He say, *I smart and one day I be rich. I love your daughter truly and she love me. She will be happy. Can I marry your daughter?*

'*No! says wise man.*

'Poor young man say, *That is your second chance. You only get three.*

'One week later he come back again. *This your last chance old man. I smart and one day I be rich. I love your daughter truly an' she love me. She will be happy. Will you let her marry me?* This time old man say yes, and they was married. The young boy a wise one, for he knows that a man needs time for Caution and Hope to set out their arguments in his mind, and main thing old man wanted was for his daughter to be happy.'

Will had opened his mouth to comment on this long-winded speech, but at that moment he caught sight of a figure coming down from the far creek bank, silhouetted against the last light in the sky.

''Hold on,' said Will. 'We've got company. He had his belt close, and slid his squirt from the leather, checking the load and walking to intercept whoever was coming towards them.

Jim went for his new Henry rifle and took up position behind a tree, ready to bear fire on any threat that might eventuate.

At the lip of the high bank, with the firelight still dancing on the knob-weed all around, Will crouched and waited. The figure, it seemed, was smaller than most men, and the broad sweep of a simple white dress was soon evident.

Will turned around, 'Stand down Jim, it's a woman by the looks of it.'

He was right. A young woman, moving with ease in bare feet on the broken surface, soon began climbing the track, pausing only to call ahead when she saw Will.

'Don't hurt me,' she called. 'I got a message.'

'No one's gonna hurt you,' said Lainey, who had hurried to meet the girl. 'Come up here an' give us your message.'

The girl arrived at the high bank, then followed Lainey over to the firelight. She was, Will judged, only about sixteen or seventeen years old.

Her skin was the colour of the night sky, and just as beautiful, her eyes liquid brown like a desert pool. Her dress was of cheap calico such as was sold or handed out in station stores around the country, but she wore it well.

Jim leaned his rifle up against a tree limb, and walked across, with his eyes kind. 'Don't be scared girl, you got nothing to fear from us. I'm from a long way east and south, Gamilaroi people.'

'Wangkumara mob,' she said, 'and thanks for lettin' my mind rest more easy.' She turned to Will. 'I work along Mister McCartney in the big house, an' he say for you to come talk with him. Bring package. Walk along me, an' I take you to him.'

Will exchanged glances with the others, then fetched not only the package, but his gun belt also, and it was only with the revolver fastened on his side that he prepared to follow the girl.

'You want me come too?' Fat Sam asked.

Will shook his head, 'Nah, leave it to me.'

★ ★ ★ ★ ★

Will and the girl spoke little as they crossed the riverbed, skirting the water and climbing the other side. From there they followed a bridle track towards the homestead, where a couple of hanging lanterns illuminated dust motes and orbiting insects.

The girl opened the front door for Will, leading him

into a drawing room, then retired deeper into the house. Joe McCartney was sitting in a leather chair, smoking a meerschaum pipe. He was lit by just one candle on a packing box table beside him. He did not rise or offer a hand, just waved his guest to a chair.

Will sat, but right on the edge of his seat. As was mentioned on his visit to the Eulo meeting room, he was not used to parking his rump on padded leather.

'I asked you to drop by,' McCartney said, 'cos you caught me wrong-footed earlier on. P'raps I was a little hasty.'

Will shrugged, deciding that hasty was one word for it. Downright rude was more apt.

'Now I appreciate that you have ridden a long way with this package, and I understand that it is addressed to me. I want to know how you came to be in possession of it.'

Will couldn't see any point lying about it. He told the story of John Clarke riding in and falling off his saddle. 'Clarkie were a mate of mine, an' I took on the task of bringin' it all this way. My crew an' I have ridden eight hundred miles. I've got traps after me in both states, and all because a' this cursed package. I'd say that's worth a hundred pound, wouldn't you?'

McCartney laid his pipe down on a bowl on the packing case. 'They's been hard seasons, these last few. You really think I'd have a hunnerd pounds sittin' around? Here's another deal, you give me the package, and tomorrow, before you ride on, you an' your mates can each swap a nag for a fresh one from the horse paddock and take away as much beef as you can carry.'

Will shook his head slowly. 'That ain't no deal. We like our own horses, and beef won't last long in this heat unless it's corned or dried.' He fiddled in his pocket for his own pipe, and McCartney threw across a packet of vestas. Will struck one on the chair leg, lit his pipe, then tossed the package back. Having drawn deeply of the smoke he said, 'Now who was this LHD, was he a mate of yours?'

'Leonard Harcourt Davies,' breathed McCartney. 'He and I have history, that's all I will say. The nerve of him to make a promise for a payment that I'm expected to keep! Typical of the man.'

Will shrugged lightly, 'Either way, a promise was made, and I intend to collect.' At that moment he recalled the story Fat Sam had told after tea. The idea had stuck in his mind. The technique of not forcing a rushed decision made sense. 'Now listen to me. Your head stockman is a good fella, an' he needs help. Tomorrow my crew are gonna go out and work the stock camp with your boys, and the next day too, so you'll get the extra value of eight man-days to sweeten things up. I've given you one chance to pay up. You've got just two more chances – tomorrer night and the next.

Then I ride away with the package and consider it mine.'

'I won't change my mind,' said McCartney.

'Maybe you will and maybe you won't,' said Will, 'but one thing's for sure.' He lifted the parcel with one hand. 'You won't see the insides of this without payin' me.'

'Go to the bloody devil,' said McCartney, between clenched teeth.

Will stood up and walked out the door, pausing only to tap his pipe out on a verandah post.

★ ★ ★ ★ ★

The following day Will, Sam, Jim and Lainey rode out early, on their own horses and packing their own tucker for the day, as they had no certainty that any would be provided for them.

Fred Chancey and his team were bringing out a mob of coachers, and Will took his place on the wings. They spent most of the morning mustering a scrubby, rocky area between a dry creek bed and a low flinty hill. Most of the cattle were happy to be driven in to the coachers, but every now and then a mad piker would take a stand.

One such animal was five feet at the shoulder, muscled like a prize-fighter with a neck like a tree trunk. He was no more fearful of the whip than of a mosquito, and when Jim and Will tried to ride him off, he turned and made the horses fearful with a wicked set of points that curved out then forwards.

It was Jim who dismounted, waited until Will had engaged the bull from the front, before running up from behind, grasping the tail and dragging down, trying to get the bull to charge back at him at the same time. Running out of legs, the bull crashed sideways to the ground, and Jim trussed him with bull-straps.

On another occasion, running out of patience, Fred Chancey shot an uncontrollable bull where it stood. 'Mean bugger anyway,' he said when it was done. 'Killed a young bull last week when it tried to make a move on 'is cows.'

During dinner camp, when Will explained to Fred Chancey how the young housemaid had come to fetch him for an audience with the boss, Fred filled them in on some of the background of the camp workers.

'That would've been Gwendoline,' he said. 'She and her sister Janey both work at the house. Local Wangkumara girls. Some of the boys are pretty good stockmen, but most of their mob got dispersed, long time back. Joe rules 'em hard, and sometimes Gwendoline or Janey gets a black eye or a bruise or two.'

At these words Jim raised his eyes, and Will saw that they were smouldering dark, filled with rage.

★ ★ ★ ★ ★

That evening when they rode back into camp, they did not take their horses to the yards to eat McCartney's precious hay. Instead, they watered them at the hole near the camp, before running them half a mile out to where Will had seen some good pick growing on the fringes of a clay pan.

'I think we should give this up, bloke,' said Jim as they watched the horses feed. 'That McCartney's a mongrel dog, an' if we stay 'ere much longer I'll do something I might regret.'

'Don't,' warned Will. 'Not unless we see it happen. Let things play out.'

Jim inclined his head, but he seemed to be anything but convinced.

★ ★ ★ ★ ★

After tea Will again buckled his gun belt on and took the package for a walk over to the homestead. The door was closed, presumably to prevent the ingress of bugs, and he knocked firmly.

It was Gwendoline who answered the door, her eyes downcast as she sat him down on the same chair as the night before, returning with Joe McCartney, still patting at his lips with his napkin.

'Late tea tonight,' he said. 'Too much to bloody do

around here. Now what do you want?'

Will lifted the package. 'A hundred pounds in cash, sir, an' I'll give you the package.'

'I've been thinking about it. I'll give you twenty guineas, a horse each and full tucker bags. That's my final offer.'

'We've got our own horses, and enough tucker to ride out. A hundred pounds is the deal. Nothing less.'

'Well, I'm not prepared to pay that,' said McCartney. 'Now get out of here.'

'You've only got one chance left,' said Will. 'After tomorrow night we'll ride away, and you'll never see us or that letter again.'

McCartney shrugged, but his eyes never left the package.

★ ★ ★ ★ ★

The following morning, assembling at the yards, when Gwendoline carried the day's tucker for the station crew across from the kitchen to the stock camp wagonette, it was obvious, even from a distance, that her lower lip had a lump of it the size of a plum, and there was a frightened and hunted look in her eye.

After she had packed the food into the boxes in the vehicle, Jim, with Will close behind, walked up close to her and examined the injury. He pointed to the homestead. 'Did that mongrel dog hit you?'

Gwendoline shook her head. 'No sir, I fell, in the dark last night.'

Will didn't believe a word of it. He had seen the girl move at night, and nary had he seen such grace from a woman or man. The idea that she might have fallen seemed ludicrous.

'You tellin' the truth there girl?' asked Jim.

Gwendoline nodded, and then she ran from both of them, away towards the homestead, hoisting her skirts and moving like the wind itself.

★ ★ ★ ★ ★

Another hard day's work followed – drier and dustier if anything than the previous day. It was an early knock-off though, for in the mid-afternoon the branding was done.

Will led his little band back to camp and looked around. 'If you lot are happy there's a good moon tonight. We'll eat, then I'd like to ride back to the Kulki and camp there. Just as soon as I've been to see old mate over at the homestead.'

Lainey looked up. 'We've all done this ride to deliver that cursed letter. Let's *all* go over there tonight, when we're packed up. Then we can leave together.'

'Fair enough,' said Will. 'That's how we'll do it then.'

Finale

WHEN EVERY pannikin and pint-pot had been scrubbed and stowed, the bedrolls buckled tight and the packs balanced, Will Jones, Fat Sam, Gamilaroi Jim and Lainey Phillips walked their plant over to the homestead and tethered them to the front fence.

Then, with Will leading the way, carrying that dead man's letter, they ascended the verandah and knocked on the door. Again, it was Gwendoline who answered, and her lip had grown more puffy through the day.

There were not enough chairs for all of them, so they entered and stood, waiting while Joe McCartney appeared.

'So, I've got the whole bloody rabble tonight, have I? So be it then, if I have to.' He sat down in his chair and lifted his pipe.

'This is your last chance,' said Will. 'One hundred pounds and the package is yours. We're ready to ride and if you don't give us the money, we're taking it with us.'

'Very well then,' McCartney sighed. 'I'll give you the money.'

At first Will could scarcely believe that he had heard correctly, but the station owner reached into his pocket and withdrew a roll of banknotes. 'One hundred pounds,' he said.

Will walked forward, one careful step at a time, still disbelieving. He stopped in front of McCartney, then reached out to take the cash with one hand, while simultaneously allowing McCartney to grip the package with the other. Each loosened their grip at the same time, and Will stepped back, hurriedly counted the notes, then stashed them in his pocket.

The station owner's face turned hard, and his voice cracked like a whip. 'You got what you wanted, now be off! I don't ever want to see your damned faces again.'

Will made no move to leave. 'If it's all the same to you, we've lived through all kinds of dangers to get this package to you. I for one would like to stay and see you open it.'

Some vestige of humour or even a love of theatre must have made the idea appeal, for McCartney slowly inclined his head. 'Stay then, and watch.' With these words he delved into his belt pouch for his knife. Again, with a sense of theatre, he used the blade to work away at the top layer of canvas.

Once this was achieved, it looked to Will like the unwrapping of a gift in a children's birthday game. The layers were thin, and well waxed. After a while it seemed that McCartney had forgotten that he had an audience, for his breath came heavy and hard, and his efforts sped up.

Beneath the canvas was another layer of a very fine cloth, and McCartney again used the knife to cut through. He grinned, 'I'm betting it's a damned fortune. It'd want to be, for all that man owes me.' He then made another long stroke with his knife.

What followed was a moment that Will would never forget. In the depths of the parcel were a multitude of what looked like yellow crystals, beautiful in the candlelight. Joe McCartney, totally engrossed now, delved his hand inside, collecting a handful of what seemed to be some kind of treasure.

Yet as soon as the crystals made contact with the air and his skin they began to smoke and steam as if by some weird magic. They spilled from his hands and the package to his lap, and something terrible must have hit his throat; surely the vapor contained in the smoke. The smell of bitter almonds permeated the room.

The station owner made a terrible sound from deep in his chest, either from pain or the recognition that the restitution of an old associate was no fortune, but some malignant trick.

Will started forward to assist, but Sam shouted, 'No, get away.' And they backed off to the far end of the room from where they watched the drama play out. Joe McCartney slipped from his chair to the floor.

Gwendoline came, alerted by the noise, standing in the doorway, her eyes wide. No one moved apart from the affected man, who began to shiver like a sufferer from the ague. No one spoke. Jim's eyes were terrible, and only Sam was calm.

Joe McCartney went into a series of spams, then curled into an untidy ball. In less than five minutes from the opening of the package he tremored for the last time and lay still.

'What the hell was it?' Will breathed, still not daring to approach the corpse.

Sam's eyes were grave, 'We Cantonese call it qíng huà wù. In the West – potassium cyanide. This was the crystal form. The fumes are what kills.'

'We've been carrying a poison all that time?' Lainey asked. 'Thank Christ we never opened the cursed thing.' Her eyes moved again to the crumpled form on the floor. 'The poor barsted. I wouldn't wish that on anyone.'

Will turned to the others. 'There's nuffink we can do here. No point in getting' involved or waiting for traps to come and start askin' questions. I reckon it's time for us to move on.'

Together they walked outside, and while the crew mounted up, Will fetched Fred Chancey from his little hut, and told him in a low voice what had happened, taking him across as far as the door, where McCartney was now pale as a sheet, and anything but peaceful.

'Sorry to leave you with a mess,' said Will. 'But we had nothing to do with it. All we done was brought the package addressed to him.

Chancey shook his head. 'Joe McCartney had a dark past. I knew it. We'll bury him tomorrow and if anyone asks, we'll say he drank too much and hit his head. Not hard to believe for those who knew him.'

Will felt no guilt, only a sense of justice that wrongs had been righted. He'd never had much education, but he'd been around enough to know that sometimes past deeds caught up to a man. He doubted there'd be many tears shed for Joe McCartney

Joining the others outside, Will mounted up and took the lead, riding off into a starlit night with his mates. There was always a new track, new places to see, and new adventures beckoning.

It was these that played in his mind as he rode.

More books by Greg Barron, all available at **ozbookstore.com**, good bookshops, and Amazon's Kindle store.

Whistler's Bones
The story of Charlie Gaunt, who rode away from his Bendigo home and joined the famous Durack cattle drive from western Queensland to the Kimberley.

The Time of Thunder
In 1990 two men from across the world, linked by history, converge on Arnhem Land in a bid to solve the fifty-year-old disappearance of a man, and to uncover a Korean War mystery that will have global ramifications.

Camp Leichhardt
Ben Mulligan went down to the Roper River fishing camp to fish for barramundi and find peace. Instead, he found himself caught in a cruel conspiracy, and ultimately fighting for his life.

Outlaw: The Story of Joe Flick
Born in the battleground between two races, Joe Flick is a promising youth. A series of incidents lead him on a path that ends in a bloody tragedy in one of the most beautiful environments on earth.

Red Jack and the Ragged Thirteen
The Ragged Thirteen were a band of thirteen larrikins who put their stamp on Australian folklore with their devil-may-care journey across the wild Northern Australian frontier.

The Last Days of Dom Sebastian
Archaeologists Francis da Costa & Nicolá Massane
follow a trail of relics & myth, uncovering a tragic love
story, and a voyage past the edge of the known world
to Australia's Kimberley.

**Galloping Jones and other True Stories from
Australia's History**
Galloping Jones was a bare-knuckle-fighting larrikin
who could tame any horse. Moondyne Joe escaped
prison using an ingenious plan that made a whole
colony laugh. Based on the popular Stories of Oz
history posts, these sketches of Australia's past will
inform and entertain you. Above all, they will remind
you of what life was like, in the days before highways
and smart phones.

All titles are available as eBooks and print copies are
always in stock at ozbookstore.com

www.ingramcontent.com/pod-product-compliance
Lightning Source LLC
Chambersburg PA
CBHW010544100726
47903CB00011B/3136